This BOOK

Bella-Mia Unit

"...CAME,
HE SAW, HE
CONKED US'!"

ANCIENT
ADVENTURES

Arms want

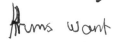

ASTONISHING ADVENTURES

Edited By Jenni Harrison

pumpoldor   wand

First published in Great Britain in 2022 by:

 Young**Writers**

Young Writers
Remus House
Coltsfoot Drive
Peterborough
PE2 9BF
Telephone: 01733 890066
Website: www.youngwriters.co.uk

Printed and bound in the UK by BookPrintingUK
Website: www.bookprintinguk.com
YB0MA0011B

FOREWORD

Are you ready to step back in time? Then come right this way - your time-travelling machine awaits! It's very simple, all you have to do is turn the page and you'll be transported to the past!

Is it magic? Is it a trick? No! It's all down to the skill and imagination of primary school pupils from around the country. We gave them the task of writing a story about any time in history, and to do it in just 100 words! I think you'll agree they've achieved that brilliantly – this book is jam-packed with exciting and thrilling tales from the past plus marvellous myths and legends along with adventures around the world.

These young authors have brought history and many things to life with their stories. This is the power of creativity and it gives us life too! Here at Young Writers we want to pass our love of the written word onto the next generation and what better way to do that than to celebrate their writing by publishing it in a book!

It sets their work free from homework books and notepads and puts it where it deserves to be – out in the world and preserved forever! Each awesome author in this book should be super proud of themselves, and now they've got proof of their imagination, their ideas and their creativity in black and white, to look back on in years to come when their first experience of publication is an ancient adventure itself!

So dive through the timelines within; you're sure to have a lot of fun. You may even learn some history facts along the way!

CONTENTS

Aldourie Primary School, Aldourie

Fletcher Devlin (8) 1

Allenby Primary School, Southall

Aroush Mahmood (9) 2

Appleton Wiske CP School, Appleton Wiske

Poppy Race (10) 3
Annabelle Race (8) 4

Avenue House School, Ealing

Clara Narezzi (9) 5
Draye Nuby (9) 6

Barnes Farm Junior School, Chelmer Village

Pranshi Mittal (9) 7

Beechwood Primary Academy, Southway

Izabela Czelny (9) 8
Lucie Pettitt (8) 9

Blackfield Primary School, Blackfield

Orla Horton (10) 10

Bolham Community Primary School, Bolham

Ava Johnson (8) 11

Britannia Community Primary School, Bacup

Molly Butterworth (8) 12
Fraser Butterworth (7) 13
Harrison Curran (8) 14
Melody James (8) 15

Broadbent Fold Primary School, Dukinfield

Mia Phillips (10) 16
Lexileigh (9) 17

Broadlands Primary School, Tupsley

Alexandra Cepoi (10) 18
Layton Door (10) 19

Buxlow Preparatory School, Wembley

Carensa Edebiri (10) 20
Aarav Gadhia (8) 21

Carrickmannon Primary School, Ballygowan

Annasophia McClintock (10)	22
Andrew Cooke (10)	23

Castle Park School, Kendal

Gracie Birkett (9)	24

Central Primary School, Port Talbot

Miranda Jones (9)	25
Avirup Panja (9)	26
Zayn Rahman (9)	27
Summer Davies (8)	28
Leynni Claire Nash (8)	29
Megan John (9)	30

Chapel Street Community Primary School, Levenshulme

Alisha Ahmed (9)	31
Alisha Imran (9)	32

Cleve House School, Knowle

Elham Pakrooh (10)	33

Edison Primary School, Heston

Amina Hassan (9)	34
Diya Mistry (9)	35
Krrish Sharma (10)	36

Everton Heath Primary School, Everton

Ruby Chipperfield (10)	37
Maisie Day (11)	38
Emily Chipperfield (11)	39
Ruby Day (10)	40

Frank Shiells (11)	41

Farringdon Academy Inspires, Farringdon

Junior Nichol (9)	42
Esme Mosebi (9)	43
Mia Gray (9)	44
Jacob Byrne (9)	45
Lilly Trotter (9)	46
Taylor Fisher (9)	47
Mia Charlton (9)	48
Harry Armour (8)	49

Galston Primary School, Galston

Amy McInally (11)	50
Neve Laverick (10)	51

Gardners Lane Primary School, Cheltenham

James Holloway (11)	52
Jed Adedipe (11)	53
Paige Jackson (11)	54
Libby Lewis-Hall (11)	55
Miley	56

Gayhurst School, Gerrards Cross

Daniel Zadeh (9)	57

Gearies Primary School, Gants Hill

Amaya Alam (9)	58
Rohit Karthikeyan (9)	59
Tanzil Ahmed (9)	60
Hudhayfah Kamran (9)	61

Giggleswick Junior School, Giggleswick

Rose Nicholson (10)	62
Oscar Dodd (9)	63
Bailey Graham (10)	64
Betsy Fairhurst (8)	65

Giggleswick Primary School, Giggleswick

Ben Brummitt (10)	66

Gosberton Academy, Gosberton

Ella Palmer (9)	67

Greensward Academy, Hockley

Bethany Stanley (11)	68
Ruby Wade (11)	69
Ellis Andrews (11)	70
Harrison Vaughan (11)	71
Jack Collier (11)	72
Elijah Conway (11)	73
Max Raymen (11)	74
Henry Waring (11)	75
Lainey Williams (11)	76

Hammond Academy, Hemel Hempstead

Olena Samantilleke (8)	77
Tobias Payne (8)	78
Dia Gutu (7)	79
Maisie Ward (7)	80
Zayef Mohammed (8)	81

Harewood Junior School, Tuffley

Grace Earl (8)	82
Giulia Mitran (8)	83
Ruby Curran (7)	84
Grace Harris (9)	85
BellaMia Unett (7)	86
Ella Bennett (9)	87
Jacob James Chambers (7)	88
Beatrice Long (8)	89
Kian Baker (8)	90
Lily Cole (9)	91

Kennoway Primary School, Kennoway

Nico Gillies/McGarrell (8)	92

Killamarsh Junior School, Killamarsh

Hollie Brayshaw (9)	93
Jack Davis (8)	94

Marden High School, North Shields

Alice Bain (11)	95

Maylandsea Primary School, Maylandsea

Sami Goolfee (8)	96

Millbank Academy, London

Caleb West (11)	97

Milton Parochial Primary School, Milton Malsor

Abigail Appleton (6)   98

Newton On Trent CE Primary School, Newton On Trent

Alexia Herberts (9)   99

Our Lady Of Lourdes Catholic Primary School, Finchley

Kai Tsui (10)   100
Michele Zeolla (9)   101
Derek Ayeni (9)   102

Parklands Primary School, Northampton

Jude Skates (9)   103
Kacey Collins (8)   104
Theo Underwood (10)   105
Elsie Roberts (10)   106

Place Farm Primary Academy, Haverhill

Anya Barrett-Prior (8)   107
Poppy Wheeler (8)   108

Ruislip Gardens Primary School, Ruislip

Bleu Cass (9)   109
Arjun Shankar (8)   110

Shade Primary School, Shade

Ashton Phillips (10)   111
Laila Harris (10)   112
Sam Knowles (10)   113
Emily Smith (9)   114
Joseph Hardcastle (10)   115

Alice Williams (9)   116
Aoife Brown (10)   117
Rhudi Warren (10)   118
Evan Bonny (10)   119
Casper Hird (10)   120
Henry Gulaiczuk (10)   121
Joseph Connor (10)   122

St Augustine Webster Catholic Primary School, Scunthorpe

Nelly Dymecka (9)   123
Victoria Skrzyszowska (10)   124

St Catherine's CE Primary School, Launceston

Martha Houlton (8)   125

St Francis Primary School, Bradford

Kaitlen Horan (9)   126
George Illingworth (8)   127

St James' CE Primary School, Oldbury

Sraiyah Williams (10)   128

St Joseph's Primary School, Gabalfa

San Aula (9)   129

St Luke's Catholic Primary School, Trench

Zarah Bernard (10)   130

St Margaret's CE Primary School, Horsforth

Joseph Hogan (10)	131
Ethan Knight (9)	132
Nancy Callaghan (10)	133

St Margaret's Primary Academy, Lowestoft

Paul Mcardle (8)	134
Abbie Attew (10)	135
Jacob Bale (11)	136
Mila Lubbock (10)	137
Joseph Knight (10)	138
Dalton Welton (11)	139
Zoe Morris (8)	140
Kaitie-Jade Stockley (9)	141
Lacie Coleman (9)	142
Oscar Cushion (10)	143

St Mark's Catholic Primary School, Great Barr

Eseosa Osayande (11)	144
Raiyaana Rehman (10)	145

St Mary's CE Primary School, Sale

Imogen Richardson (9)	146

St Michael's CE Primary School, Bolton

Aima Waqar (9)	147
Mahnoor Khan (9)	148

St Paul's CE Junior School, Kingston Upon Thames

Issacisla Hayman (9)	149

St Sebastian's RC Primary School, Douglas Green

Talha Ahmad (10)	150

Starbeck Primary Academy, Starbeck

Abigail Snodgrass (10)	151

Temple Mill Primary School, Strood

Leanna Holl (9)	152
Luke Gorham (9)	153
Esmai Pook (8)	154
Poppy Cobb (9)	155

The Bishops' CE Learning Academy, Treninnick Hill

Jesse McIntosh (11)	156
Summer Crowther (11)	157
Stanley Richardson (11)	158
Samuel Rawsthorn (11)	159
Miley Hill (10)	160
Maja Abram (10)	161
Izak Lategan (10)	162

The Godolphin Junior Academy, Slough

Fatimah Khan (9)	163

The King's House School, Windsor

Gabriella Swart (9)	164
Nathaniel Bramley (9)	165

Tudor Primary School, Southall

Muhammed Hassan Saeed (11)	166
Safina Yakub (10)	167

Walgrave Primary School, Walgrave

Finn Campbell (11)	168

Washingborough Academy, Washingborough

Katy-May Adair (11)	169

Whitburn Village Primary School, Whitburn

Isla Gael Martin (9)	170

Wyburns Primary School, Rayleigh

Izzy Sampson (8)	171
Harry Dodd (8)	172
Hayden Aylott (9)	173
Isla Brindle (8)	174
Phoebe Glendinning (8)	175
Hayden R (8)	176
Chloe Day (8)	177
Kiki Howell (9)	178
Tommy Mackenzie (8)	179
Ivy Newcombe	180
Sydnee Herrera (9)	181
Kamil Quereshi (9)	182
George (8)	183

THE MINI SAGAS

Time Travelling Julius Caesar

I was heading into battle, then I teleported. I woke up in a testing lab. I was stuck in a glass test tube. "I can't get out!" In front of me were two aliens. I turned my back to the aliens. As I turned around I spotted an opening. I managed to crawl through. I was free at last. I ran and ran until I found a time machine. I tried to figure how to control it. I managed to teleport myself back to 100 BC. I won the battle and many more. I went on five more adventures.

Fletcher Devlin (8)
Aldourie Primary School, Aldourie

The Treasure In The Pyramid

In the sandy, scorching desert with beautiful pyramids. Inside the pyramid there was some special treasure, but I couldn't go inside because of the scary mummies. Surrounding the pyramid were mummies. I tried to distract them, but I was not able to. All of a sudden, my friends came. I don't know how they distracted them. Meanwhile, I sneakily went to the other side. I went inside. It was boiling hot, even hotter than before. Sweat was dripping down my face quickly. I finally saw the golden treasure. I ran out and I told everyone I got the treasure!

Aroush Mahmood (9)
Allenby Primary School, Southall

Shadow

Ryder panted. After stealing Alexander the Great's gold, he was out of breath. After he locked the door, it dawned on him the guards had followed him. He waited silently in infinite darkness.

Knock, knock. Ryder held his breath. The guards burst the door open and the noise they created was overwhelming, like someone being murdered in a cave.

Alexander marched in. The sun blinded Ryder. As they tied his hands behind his back, tears welled up in his eyes. "I wish I could go back!" Suddenly, everything went black.

Next thing he knew he was in Alexander's money safe...

Poppy Race (10)
Appleton Wiske CP School, Appleton Wiske

Anna The Slave

There was a little girl called Anna. She was a slave working in a palace for a king named King Pin. She wished to go to school like all the other children. She didn't think it was fair.

One night, she was going to bed. She wished not to be a slave.

The next morning, it came true. She went to the palace. King Pin said another person was working for her. She was so happy she started a school and she loved it. She was really smart and she made lots of friends. She loved to play lots.

Annabelle Race (8)
Appleton Wiske CP School, Appleton Wiske

4

Lauren And Zedd

Long ago on the island of Crete somebody called Zedd wanted power and money. He told Lauren, his sister and Lauren exclaimed, "The scriptures have all the ingredients you will need!"
Zedd searched and searched but didn't find the scriptures. Zedd thought that Lauren had played a prank so he tried to revenge on her. However, Lauren was smart. She knew what was going to happen. Zedd pretended to make the scriptures. He looked everywhere to find a spell but Lauren tried it out on Zedd and he turned to stone but Lauren was happy forever.

Clara Narezzi (9)
Avenue House School, Ealing

The King And The Monster

A long time ago in a country called Greece, there was a very strong king called Max. He was very powerful so was his country but one day a monster wanted to defeat the king and the entire city. But the king was too powerful for him. The king went outside to fight the monster. The king had a sword and bow and arrow. The monster was using his teeth to swallow him. The king chopped his head off and ran away. The monster was dead and they lived a happy life together.

Draye Nuby (9)
Avenue House School, Ealing

The Fear Of Crossing

It takes an eternity to cross no-man's-land. I begin to wonder if we'll ever find their trenches at all. Then we see their wire up ahead. We wriggle through a gap, and still undetected, we drop down into their trench. I notice their trench is much deeper than ours, wider too and altogether firmer than ours. It looks deserted but we know it can't be. We still hear the voices and the music. I grip my rifle tighter and follow the others along the trench, bent double like everyone else. My heart sinks as I see our enemies.

Pranshi Mittal (9)
Barnes Farm Junior School, Chelmer Village

The Stake

It struck 6 o'clock.

"Burn her!" they chanted.

"No, you have to listen, please. Argh!" said a woman as she was lit up in flames. It was nearly my turn. Sweat was dripping down my body. I had 10 minutes left to live, they thought I was a witch.

"Next!"

I walked to the stake. They tied me to the stake. Was this all because I had a black cat or because I was a healer? I looked down at my feet and saw all the ashes. I froze in shock. Then he took the match out.

"Please, no..."

Izabela Czelny (9)
Beechwood Primary Academy, Southway

A Girl Dreaming About Having Glasses

One day a girl went to sleep. She had a dream about having glasses. She lived in ancient Egypt. She liked it there.

She found another girl called Loler. Loler was being mean to her, she was being extremely mad. Liler was sad. Loler felt sorry so she said sorry. So they became friends. But Loler had no one to live with so she lived with Liler.

Then Liler woke up. She saw it was a dream. She was relieved and happy.

Lucie Pettitt (8)
Beechwood Primary Academy, Southway

The Scientist And The Machine

One normal day, there was a scientist who loved to experiment. But one day she had made this weird machine but did not want to test it out. No one did. Everyone was shocked when the scientist finally agreed to do it. She stepped into the machine and *boom!* She was in London but there was fire! People screaming! It was the Great Fire of London. She ran. She was petrified. There was no way out. "Why did I decide to go into the machine?" The fire was heading towards her. It was getting closer and closer...

Orla Horton (10)
Blackfield Primary School, Blackfield

The Trouble With Building Pyramids

Once upon a time in ancient Egypt, there were ten men building the pyramids for the king. Five of the men were called Helpful and the other five were called Really Helpful. As they were building the pyramids, the Really Helpful men realised that the blocks were made out of sand which made sense why the blocks kept falling apart. The Helpful men had the bright idea of adding water to the sand so it would stick together better. After the men added the water to the sand they could build the pyramid. It took twenty years to build.

Ava Johnson (8)
Bolham Community Primary School, Bolham

Hadrian's Wall

Hadrian ordered his servants to build him a big wall around Rome itself. The servants couldn't agree on a colour. One wanted pale, another wanted red. Nobody could agree so it turned into an argument then fighting and punching. They had a fallout. When Hadrian heard the noise he stormed into the room.

"What is this noise? I only want red!" he yelled.

"Let's get started then," said one of the servants.

But one still wasn't happy. He wanted revenge very very badly. So he got revenge on Hadrian's wall.

Molly Butterworth (8)
Britannia Community Primary School, Bacup

Hadrian's Wall

We were going to attack Caledonia. When we got there, nobody was seen. We had a look around Caledonia until our leader shouted us over. We realised one of us was missing. We looked for him. I found his body lying there. I told the others. We looked again but this time we were in twos. I noticed that my partner was gone. I thought it was an ambush. I got to the others and we all decided to make a wall. We got to work on Hadrian's wall. It took five days.

Fraser Butterworth (7)
Britannia Community Primary School, Bacup

Hadrian's Wall

We were the Romans, one of the strongest tribes in the world. The Celts kept bothering us so we built Hadrian's wall to protect us from them.
We went to work. We were tired but that didn't stop us. We were nowhere near finishing but we never stopped. Brick by brick, step by step, I knew we would finish it. I was super tired but I pushed on so we could finish. The Celts were not getting past this. I was 100% sure they wouldn't.

Harrison Curran (8)
Britannia Community Primary School, Bacup

Romans And Celts

The Celts were working hard for Boudicca.
A few days later, the Romans invaded the Celts'
home. Boudicca shouted and all the Celts rushed
to fight against them. Boudicca was fighting like
she had never fought before.
A little girl sat on her windowsill. She said to her
father, "I want to be like Boudicca.
Her dad said, "When you are older."

Melody James (8)
Britannia Community Primary School, Bacup

The Time-Travelling Egyptian Mystery

I suddenly heard something strange coming from the necklace! My heart was beating hard, like a thousand drums banging together loudly! Wind swirled everywhere. I yelped and tried to grab Coco to keep her safe. I could see all of the stairs spinning around dizzily, but after that, it went black! I felt the spinning starting to slow down. I landed with my eyes still closed. With a flash, my eyes opened. "Where are we?" I asked.

Coco pulled to get closer to the pyramid. I was so puzzled. Why were people wearing those strange outfits? I thought really hard...

Mia Phillips (10)
Broadbent Fold Primary School, Dukinfield

My Mysterious Egyptian Time Lapse

It was an ordinary day. My mum, my brother and I were walking home from school and when we got home, I went to my room. I was playing games on my iPad, but today was no ordinary day. I was enjoying playing my Harry Potter game when I smelt a horrible smell. I looked at it. It was glowing brightly and hurting my eyes. I found a glass on the floor and picked it up. It was glowing. Suddenly, I got sucked in. I woke up and I was somewhere else, I was in Egypt.

Lexileigh (9)
Broadbent Fold Primary School, Dukinfield

The Lost Queen

As soon as everyone saw the alien, they started to run. The alien went to the Queen's house.
When he got inside, the alien kidnapped the queen and went to his rocket and to space. When the alien got to space, he put the queen in the basement. Then he got dressed in the queen's dress.
The alien went back to the castle and everyone thought that he was the queen but the maid saw it wasn't the queen. More and more people started disappearing.
The alien went back to space to get the queen but the queen had vanished.

Alexandra Cepoi (10)
Broadlands Primary School, Tupsley

The Dinosaur Life

The forest felt like soft pillows under Johny's feet. Lots of dinosaurs were rushing to Johny because they were his friend. A hunter came and scouted the area for any vicious beasts. Johny saw the hunter and got all the dinosaurs hidden away. Johny saw the hunter and tried to run away. The hunter got closer and closer. Finally, he got Johny. He tried to convince Johny to tell him where the dinosaurs were but out of the corner of his eye, he saw a dinosaur. The hunter sadly killed the dinosaur.

Layton Door (10)
Broadlands Primary School, Tupsley

Zeus' Children

From the sky, I was watching below, until one of my helpers told me someone wanted to see me. "Tell Poseidon I'm busy."
"Sire, it's not Poseidon who's at the door, it's a boy and girl requesting to see you."
I was very confused because I lived in the sky, only a god could get here.
I went to take a look and when I opened the door I saw two children looking very excited to see me.
"Father, we have finally found you!"
"Children, it's you! But how did you get here?"
"Father, let me explain..."

Carensa Edebiri (10)
Buxlow Preparatory School, Wembley

The Forbidden Mummy

A mummy named Felix got revived twenty years after his mummification in Mumbai, India. He regained his memory and found himself alive. As he was looking for ages, he finally found shelter and decided to spend the night there.

The next day, a kind man approached and shared his house.

That night, he was trying to sleep while spirits were putting a spell on him.

The next day, he found himself outside the house face down. He soon found out the spirits had cursed him.

Felix went to a therapist. The therapist gave him a potion, the curse was removed.

Aarav Gadhia (8)
Buxlow Preparatory School, Wembley

Evacuee

Mother had dressed me in my neatest clothes and sent me to the station with Papa. The station had never been so busy. Papa had brought my case and a corned beef sandwich for the journey. I spotted my friend Mary Tucker and greeted her. Mary looked pale and kept wiping her brow with a silk handkerchief and tugging her mother's embroidered apron. Finally, Papa waved me off and said to write lots. We were rushed onto the train and seated immediately. I felt a tear trickle down my cheek. Mary hugged me and we shared her toffees together.

Annasophia McClintock (10)
Carrickmannon Primary School, Ballygowan

Emu Wars

During the great depression, Australia was not good. A lot of their soldiers turned into farmers. Now the emus were doing their routine but now there were nice crops to eat and other animals were eating the remains. Then the military were involved, killing emus, but they couldn't kill a single one. After a few months they were killing hundreds but the government was not happy. So far the emus had won every battle even though they were killing hundreds. To fix the whole thing they just made better fences!

Andrew Cooke (10)
Carrickmannon Primary School, Ballygowan

Funny Mummy

In the beginning there was a mummy that found herself in a funny world with funny-looking people. They were funny-looking people because they wore clothes instead of bandages. She felt like she didn't belong in this non-bandged world. Suddenly, she walked into a shop and started putting on clothes, but it didn't go well. She had shorts on her head and T-shirts on her arms and shoes on her face. But after some silliness, she thought to herself, *I'm better off in bandages than silly clothes*. She went back to where she belonged.

Gracie Birkett (9)
Castle Park School, Kendal

Cleopatra And Miranda

One morning, I saw gold smoke. Then I saw a girl with brown eyes and brown hair wearing a pharaoh dress. She started talking but I didn't understand so I used my hands. She was interested in my clothes. I said, "My name is Miranda."
She said her name was Cleopatra. My mum was calling so I said goodbye.
When I got home, Cleopatra was gone, along with my favourite clothes and Nike shoes! But she'd left a special rock.
A week later, the school went on a trip to Egypt. Cleopatra was there wearing my shoes and favourite top!

Miranda Jones (9)
Central Primary School, Port Talbot

Hunting Of Pharaoh Tutankhamun

In ancient Egypt, there was a famous pharaoh called Tutankhamun. He became pharaoh at the age of nine. He loved hunting very much.
One day, Pharaoh Tutankhamun went to the bank of the River Nile to hunt fish. But he didn't know that some fierce crocodiles and hippos lived there. He was on his raft in the River Nile, trying to hunt a large fish. Unfortunately, a huge, dangerous hippo headed toward him and chomped the raft into pieces. Pharaoh Tutankhamun shouted for help. At that time, his bodyguards came and rescued him.

Avirup Panja (9)
Central Primary School, Port Talbot

What Are Mummies?

The practice of preserving a body as a mummy was worldwide throughout time. It took 70 days to prepare the corpse before it went in the tomb. They prepared the body by washing it, removing all the organs, except the heart, and placing them in jars. They then packed the body and organs in salt to remove moisture. They embalmed the body with resins and essential oils such as myrrh, cassia, juniper oil and cedar oil and wrapped the embalmed corpse in several layers of linen. Basically, a mummy is a dead human or animal.

Zayn Rahman (9)
Central Primary School, Port Talbot

Lia's Viking Story

Once upon a time, there was a girl called Lia, with her mom. They moved to Norway but when they got there, nobody was there. They walked to a shelter. When they were there, they met Thor, the Viking god.

Thor said, "Follow me to a wonderful place."

But it wasn't wonderful. There was a Viking battle. Thor gave them weapons to fight. It ended in a tie.

Thor said, "Let's have a Viking feast with everyone."

Everyone said, "Let's have a Viking day!"

Summer Davies (8)

Central Primary School, Port Talbot

The Tomb's Curse

It was a sunny afternoon in the deserts of Egypt.
An explorer named Bob Smith was getting ready to
explore Tutankhamun's tomb.
When he entered, he felt a sudden shake in the
ground. He started to panic as rocks began to fall
from the ceiling of the tomb. Items began to fall
from their places. That's when Bob realised that the
tomb was collapsing. Bob had nowhere to go and
he thought that it was going to end in disaster...
Then Bob woke up and realised it was all a
nightmare!

Leynni Claire Nash (8)
Central Primary School, Port Talbot

The Viking

Once upon a time, there was a Viking. His name was Bob. His sister's name was Vexy. Both had blue eyes and brown hair. They were good Vikings but then the Saxons had a plan to stop the Vikings. They built a wall but the wall was stone so the Vikings couldn't get through it. Vexy had a plan to get through it.
Two years later, they got through with a brick ship to attack them.
In 2,000AD, they stopped attacking. Vexy and Bob started to live happily ever after.

Megan John (9)
Central Primary School, Port Talbot

Sophia Captured By The Romans

Sophia was a girl who lived in India. She had a great personality. After her mother died, she started to live alone. Sophia was 16 and travelled with her mom, Lidia.

She stopped travelling for a while after her mother died. Then the incident happened. She decided to travel to Egypt on a boat. After a while, a boat behind her started chasing her. The men had weapons and armour. They came onto Sophia's boat and took her away. These men were called Romans. They took her to Rome.

Alisha Ahmed (9)
Chapel Street Community Primary School, Levenshulme

The Girl Who Lived In Ancient Times

Once a lovely girl named Liab was strolling in the jungle that she loved. She never knew how dangerous it could be in the jungle. She saw something weird up in a tree. It was black. What could it be? She got out her spear, sword and shield. In one shot, she threw her spear and the thing fell down as quick as a flash. She found it and took it to her mother. Her mother was surprised and told her it was a stole. They lived happily ever after!

Alisha Imran (9)
Chapel Street Community Primary School, Levenshulme

A Rotten Roman Romance

I'm the Queen of Egypt. I'm married to my brother. Over the world, people admire my beauty, but they are missing my intellect.

I disposed of my first brother with Caesar's help. My brother is at the bottom of the Nile. I've been married to another brother, I'll have to devise his demise.

I plan to woo Caesar. I'll wrap myself up in a carpet and emerge in his bed chamber like an Egyptian goddess. He couldn't resist that. Two birds, one stone; Caesar will help kill my brother. Get rid of my brother, marry Caesar.

Elham Pakrooh (10)
Cleve House School, Knowle

The Best Designer In Egypt

Once upon a time, there was a girl called Chione. She was the best designer in ancient Egypt. Every time there was a competition she would win. One day, Chione entered another competition but so did her sister. Her sister's name was Tauret. She was a designer too but had stopped. It would be hard.

As they started the competition, Chione was unfocused and kept thinking about Tauret. She turned and saw all of Egypt cheering. She could do it!

As it finished, the judges announced who the best designer was... Chione and Tauret were scared. But it was Chione.

Amina Hassan (9)
Edison Primary School, Heston

The Night Of The Mummy

One night, there was a crack in one of the mummy's coffins. Later that night. it escaped and got loose in the museum. It destroyed everything. In the morning, as the people walked in, they were astonished by what had happened. All of a sudden, the mummy ran out of the museum and caused chaos in the city. Everyone was running wild and the police couldn't handle them. Instead, the police tried to handle the mummy. It took lots of tired legs and hands but they did it.

After, they put it back in the coffin safe and sound.

Diya Mistry (9)
Edison Primary School, Heston

The War...

A long time ago, there was a king called Black Darkness. He was the king of the Underworld. He always wanted to take revenge on the Overworld for locking him underground.
Once, one of his scouts reported to the king that he'd heard people from the overground talking about what they were going to do if the demon king attacked them. The king ordered his largest soldier to break out and it worked. A massive war had begun. In the end, the only person that was still standing was the demon lord...

Krrish Sharma (10)
Edison Primary School, Heston

Burning

8th June 793, Lindisfarne was burning! It was a Viking raid. My head spun as the Vikings stole the monks' property and cowardly ran away to their massive, sleek dragon-like ship. We all watched in horror as they hobbled into their boats and picked up immensely oversized oars, banging them on the wooden, wet sides of the ship, before sailing away on the smooth, glossy surface of the water. The ship elegantly cut through the waves like a sharp knife going through raw meat. The crackling behind us was unbearably deafening, but the monks crying in horror was much louder.

Ruby Chipperfield (10)
Everton Heath Primary School, Everton

The Knights

The knighthood were heavily armoured soldiers who rode on horseback. Only the wealthiest nobles could offer to be a knight. At Christmas, they ate raw eggs and pigs' heads. Knights wore metal armour and metal plates in their jackets. The knight was a person granted an honorary title of knighthood or representative of service to the military capacity. Knighthood finds its origins in the Greek hippies and hoplite and Roman eques and constitution of classical antiquity. In the early, middle ages in Europe, knighthood was conferred upon Anointed warriors.

Maisie Day (11)
Everton Heath Primary School, Everton

The Holocaust

In Bergen-Belsen on the 7th of February, I contracted Typhus... a deadly disease. Typhus kills you after twelve days of contracting the disease. During those twelve days, I grew weaker and weaker because of the illness. Margot too. The day before I got Typhus, my mother died of starvation. The work and bad conditions kept it off my mind. One night, I woke up to a loud crash; Margot had fallen out of her high bed. Weakened by the disease, she unfortunately died. I woke up to the loud crash and being as weak as I was, died from shock.

Emily Chipperfield (11)
Everton Heath Primary School, Everton

King Henry VIII

Henry went on lots of dates. He had six wives. He established the Church of England and the Royal Navy. Henry VIII came to the throne when his father, Henry VII, died on 21 April 1509. He was a powerful man and a charismatic figure; perhaps best known for his tumultuous love life and the establishment of the Church of England. Henry was born at Greenwich Palace on 28 June 1491 and died on 28 January 1547. He lived in Hampton Court, the City of London and Windsor Castle. He was seventeen when he became king.

Ruby Day (10)
Everton Heath Primary School, Everton

The Spitfire Pilot

I am Tony. I fly a Submarine Spitfire in World War II. I have been through a lot. Once, I fell out of the air into a free fall. I managed to eject. My Spitfire crash-landed but I managed to get to safety. Unfortunately, my friend died in the middle of landing, meaning I was given his Spitfire. It was brand spanking new. I managed to knock a few Germans out, using lots of missiles. Throughout my career, I bombed lots of places as well, leaving many casualties and grieving families.

Frank Shiells (11)
Everton Heath Primary School, Everton

The Mummy And The Brave Explorer

There once was a mummy who had someone on the other side. Everyone was scared of him except Jake, he was an explorer. At first, the mummy thought that Jake was gonna run away but he didn't. All he did was stare at the mummy.
The mummy finally spoke. He asked, "Me need help." Jake pulled the mummy into his van. The mummy told him all about it.
Hours later they arrived at the dragon's ruin. They saw the potion. They sprinted towards it. But the dragon came down. Jake held the dragon off. The mummy transformed into a human.

Junior Nichol (9)
Farringdon Academy Inspires, Farringdon

The Girl Who Is Friends With A Dragon

One day, there was an eighteen-year-old. She was named Katie. She loved dragons and she wanted one as a friend... But one day her dream came true! She woke up to a strange noise coming from under her bed. She got up, bent down and saw a dragon. The dragon suddenly spoke. "Hello, Katie. My name is Daniel!" explained the dragon. Katie's jaw dropped.

A couple of years later... the dragon was coughing like crazy. Katie was so worried. She kept giving him medicine. Then he suddenly passed out. Katie went to see if he was breathing...

Esme Mosebi (9)
Farringdon Academy Inspires, Farringdon

Vampire Invasion

It was nightfall. Ancient vampires lurked but it was time they came to an end. The vampire hunter came out with sixteen stakes laced with vervain. A vampire jumped out at her. She staked it in the heart. She ran away as more vampires chased her. She shot at them with wooden bullets. They wouldn't hold them for long. Before she knew it, hundreds of vampires came. Even her bullets weren't enough. She had to chop off their heads, stake them, give them vervain, anything to survive. She cheered, "All the vampires are gone! Yay!"

Mia Gray (9)
Farringdon Academy Inspires, Farringdon

The End Of Ghosts

One day, a mysterious ship docked at a Viking town. This ship belonged to an army of ghosts. The Vikings knew this so they ordered for warriors to be sent.
After some days they didn't return. Then Harold ordered for 300 warriors to be sent. They didn't return. That same night the houses vanished.
The Vikings had an idea so they sang a song while waving around fire. They thought the ghosts would retreat. They were correct and the next day the ship was gone. The Vikings had a huge celebration. That celebration lasted two days.

Jacob Byrne (9)
Farringdon Academy Inspires, Farringdon

The Viking In Danger

There was a Viking called Elsta but he used to get called El and he drank poisons that were really dangerous! He had no family, nothing. He was on his own for his whole life. Nobody loved him. Also he never once got told to stop drinking poisons. He was a strong, brave boy. He never ate or drank anything. All he had was gone. Until somebody found him drinking a poison so she said, "What you drinking?"
So he said, "My poison?"
"Well you shouldn't be drinking them, they are really really dangerous!"

Lilly Trotter (9)
Farringdon Academy Inspires, Farringdon

The Viking Kings

Once upon a time, there was a skeleton army attacking a village and all of the Vikings attacked the skeleton army. The children were hiding in a building and watched their parents kill the army. The next day, another army of skeletons attacked their village again. Then the children killed the skeletons while their parents were asleep in bed. When their parents woke up the children told their parents that they killed the skeletons. Then they moved villages, away from their old village so the skeleton army could not find them.

Taylor Fisher (9)
Farringdon Academy Inspires, Farringdon

The Lost Mummy

One day, a mummy went outside to see his friend but his friend was not there. So he went to look in the forest. He looked for hours and then decided to leave, but he was lost. The mummy thought it was going to be fine so he looked around until it had been a day. The mummy found a trail and followed it. He followed it for an hour then the track led him to the exit. The mummy was so happy.
Then his friend came and they had lunch at the mummy's house and had much fun.

Mia Charlton (9)
Farringdon Academy Inspires, Farringdon

The Mythic Potion

Once upon a time, there was a time in Rome. There was a Viking who was always thinking about the mythic potion to make him twice the power. To get it you had to slay a beast. To get it there were two decisions to make: they were to slay the beast or to go unseen to get it from him. He chose to go unseen and slay him.

He broke the decision. He was now determined to kill that beast by getting the potion to kick him off a 500m cliff to die.

Harry Armour (8)
Farringdon Academy Inspires, Farringdon

Annie Clover The Outlaw

On a dark, lonely night, I heard a fearful scream. At first, I thought nothing of it, but the next day I was sobbing. My best friend had gone missing! I tried to tell the sheriff but he didn't care because in our town people always went missing. "Go home, little girl," the sheriff told me. I was only ten after all. I found a clover, hoping it was lucky.

Years later she was never found... I was so mad I killed the sheriff and ran to get revenge. Then, that's how I became Annie Clover, the most famous outlaw!

Amy McInally (11)

Galston Primary School, Galston

No-Good Neve

Howdy, I'm No-Good Neve. When I was ten I had no family, they were killed. So I decided I was going to get revenge, starting with school. At lunch I escaped and got on my horse. I went to my uncle and got a gun. When I was riding on my horse and saw a map I followed the map and met people my age that were outlaws too. We became friends. We robbed trains and banks. But one day I had a stand-off and I was about to win but then *bang! Crack! Snap!* Everything went black.

Neve Laverick (10)
Galston Primary School, Galston

The Tale Of Blackbeard

Another day, another raid and killing crewmates who didn't show enough devotion to me. We were raiding ships for sugar, one day when suddenly, one of my best pirates was slain. I went absolutely crazy! I killed everyone on the ship.

That evening, I realised I was running out of men so the next day, I enslaved some more pirates.

That evening, I woke up to a sword at my throat. I heard those traitors say, "This is what you deserve for what you did to us!"

Then I got slayed but I assure you... I shall return.

James Holloway (11)
Gardners Lane Primary School, Cheltenham

The Night Of The Murderous Black Spot

One stormy night, there was a crewmate that was worried about something called the Black Spot. His friend spotted him and they talked. The crewmate started panicking when he saw different black spots. He shivered in fear as he was talking to his friend. Eventually, he hadn't realised that his friend was the real Black Spot. As he left, the captain of the ship was waiting behind the door. The crewmate didn't notice that the captain was behind the door. As he opened and closed the door, the captain killed him permanently.

Jed Adedipe (11)
Gardners Lane Primary School, Cheltenham

Stealing Back

Ten years I've been searching, discovering new things. Not one has been a soul without a body. Sending letters every hour of the day. Not even two have reached him. I am the poorest on land, now he's done this. Most days I just plan on my ship. Other days, I just boss my crew around. Don't give up hope because I will find this pirate thief soon. Pull the strings. Fire the cannons. Start the boat. Send the letters. Hold the guns. Invade the ship. Kill the guards. Sink the ships. Find the captain. Sail far away.

Paige Jackson (11)
Gardners Lane Primary School, Cheltenham

Blackbeard's Crew!

Bang! went the captain's gun.

"No Ace!"

Without thinking, I screamed at the top of my lungs.

"Ace, you wicked man. How could you? He was loyal!"

Blackbeard's eyes slowly turned to meet mine. I stared intensely into his eyes. Quickly, I snatched his powerful gun and pointed it at him. Blackbeard's eyes turned to meet mine. He was confused but amazed at what I could do. I pulled the trigger. *Bang!*

Libby Lewis-Hall (11)

Gardners Lane Primary School, Cheltenham

Blackbeard's Death

This was it. The chance to defeat Blackbeard was upon us. It was us against him. No getting away this time. I'd figured out a plan. I just had to tell the crew.

"He's coming. Quick! Get in position!"

Bang! He was dead. What did this mean? We had done it. Our plan had been a success. Did this mean all the treasure would go to us so we could go home?

Miley
Gardners Lane Primary School, Cheltenham

Shambled In Shadows

I approached the room, clenched in shackles. It felt like my veins were disintegrating. Blood spilling, the chains tightened their grip, making me suffer. The doors swung open, the breeze froze my red dripping blood. My skin turned deep purple. Thereafter, I was suffocating and my blood was boiling like it was in a saucepan. 'Twas like my brain had been gouged out. Ravenously trying to break free, I closed the curtains of my eyes. A tingling sensation shuddered down my spine as I struggled, eyes shut tight, but suddenly a dark, gloomy feeling overcame me, an infinite black hole.

Daniel Zadeh (9)
Gayhurst School, Gerrards Cross

Going To Londinium

There was a girl named Melody. She was 19 years old. She loved to make things. One evening, she made an astonishing invention. It was a time machine. When Melody showed her parents they were amazed. She travelled back to her 16th birthday party but something went wrong. Melody had gone back to Roman times!
When she got there, she was confused but she realised where she was. Melody looked around. She spotted Roman soldiers shoving citizens around. She wanted to help. Brave Melody stood up to the soldiers. After, she ran back to her machine and safely got home.

Amaya Alam (9)
Gearies Primary School, Gants Hill

A Brave Soldier

A boy named Atti wanted to be a Roman soldier when he grew up. He got his wish but it turned into a disaster because the new emperor, Nero, was impolite to his subjects. Atti and his legion wanted to destroy Nero.

Ten months later, Atti's legion's cook got to make a feast for the emperor as his mum had come. Atti told the cook to poison just the emperor's food. Atti went and blended in with the guards. Nero called Atti over because he was unwell. They went to his room and Nero fainted. He died and everyone celebrated.

Rohit Karthikeyan (9)
Gearies Primary School, Gants Hill

The Fight Of Heroism And Villainy

As Neli wandered around the abandoned ancient castle, he looked around. An evil creature, called a Zetsu, struck him. Luckily, he defeated it. Then a big, evil legendary warrior, named Kaguya, ambushed Neli. Kaguya was very powerful. Neli came pouncing out but Kaguya was so quick she dodged his fists. He kept attacking and she would carry on dodging him. He managed to get a hit. He blocked her energy point so she wasn't as strong. Then he hit her once, then again. He hit her so many times that she was defeated. Neli became a hero.

Tanzil Ahmed (9)
Gearies Primary School, Gants Hill

The Crystal In The Forest

Once upon a time, there was a boy called Jay. He was from a very poor family. One day, he went out for a walk with his dog, called Jack, through a forest. As they walked through the deep green forest, Jack saw something glistening and ran towards it. Jay ran after Jack and did not see the ditch. He was running and fell in. Jack came back with a crystal in his mouth and found Jay in the ditch. Jack grabbed a rope from home and came back and rescued Jay.

They sold the crystal and became millionaires!

Hudhayfah Kamran (9)
Gearies Primary School, Gants Hill

Run Away

I ran. I ran harder than I have ever run before. So hard I swear there was a mini earthquake every time my feet hit the ground. They were behind me with their dreadful whips and their scowling faces. The concentration camp, I couldn't go back... Suddenly, they had me. I tried to squirm but it was no use. Then my mother appeared from the smoke. "I thought you were dead!" I screamed. For I had wept for days over her supposed loss. But she didn't respond. Instead, she knocked out both of the guards. I ran... She didn't follow.

Rose Nicholson (10)
Giggleswick Junior School, Giggleswick

1914... War!

It's hard surviving the war. Every day at least five soldiers get killed! The food isn't that good, we only have canned food. We're all trying to hold off all of the nasty, dangerous, ferocious German soldiers. All the kids were heartbroken when they heard that they were going away from their parents and their dads were going to war! We're losing soldiers. The Germans are coming near our base, we need to get the rest of our men to fight back, we don't care if they're not trained for this! We need somebody to get more men, please.

Oscar Dodd (9)
Giggleswick Junior School, Giggleswick

Life In London

James and I were walking home from school. We had saved up all our pocket money for this moment, the best ice cream shop ever! All of a sudden, a strange lady jumped out at us and started screaming, "How could you be so stupid?" I had no idea why she was shouting so much. Then I realised she'd saved us, but James being James, ran. I never listened to my brother, it was a good job too. Next thing I knew, there was a *bang, bang* noise. The Germans... That was the last I ever saw of my brother.

Bailey Graham (10)
Giggleswick Junior School, Giggleswick

The Two Guns

A British soldier was waiting for ages for some movement from the Germans. He drank a full bottle of water so he needed to go to the toilet, but the bad thing was that he went off duty and Winston Churchill saw him. Then he found a guy below! "Hi," the man said, "do you know where the toilet is?" They got out their guns and one man shot the other man...

Betsy Fairhurst (8)
Giggleswick Junior School, Giggleswick

The Plague

Many years ago, a large old rat lived in the dark alleys of London. One morning, he was out looking for food when suddenly an old lady with a black boil on her elbow shouted, "Rat!" So he scurried away and hid behind an old cart.

When it was safe he carefully poked his nose out and checked the coast was clear. Without any warning, he heard loud crackling and smelt burning. As he got closer he saw a huge fire spreading across the streets of London. He trembled with fear as the flames came toward him.

Ben Brummitt (10)
Giggleswick Primary School, Giggleswick

Girl Magic

On a hot sunny day, three girls were walking through the woods whilst on a Brownie scavenger hunt. They were surprised to find what appeared to be a really old black magic cookbook. They couldn't decide if they should give it to Andy, the Brownie leader or take it into their own hands. Eventually, they decided to return the book back to the camp and hide in their tent. They started reading out the spells and were amazed at what they read. They photographed the recipes in the book and hid it again for another Brownie to find and enjoy.

Ella Palmer (9)
Gosberton Academy, Gosberton

The Storm Struck

Centuries ago, the hot flaming sun shone down on the people, it was a very hot summer's day. The next day, a storm came upon them. There was an old lady that lived in a house away from the village. Her roof was a bit old so it fell down when lightning struck her home. She got up, panting frantically. She ran upstairs and hid under her bed. She waited and then her house collapsed and she was stuck. She couldn't move. It was dark and she heard something. She shouted, "Help!" Men lifted the bed. The storm had gone.

Bethany Stanley (11)
Greensward Academy, Hockley

World War II

Sitting inside the bomb shelter, terrified, the sounds of bombs exploding and guns firing and children screaming was just heartbreaking to hear. Seeing people suffer in pain or from losing a loved one. Soldiers were putting their lives at risk just to save strangers and loved ones in their community. It just shows that one person can make a huge difference. No one would want to experience what we were all going through. Let's just say rest in peace to all the people who passed away during the upsetting times of World War II.

Ruby Wade (11)
Greensward Academy, Hockley

The Beach Viking

There he sat alone, afraid. A Viking far from home, the sun beaming down on the sandy beach that gently tickled his toes. The wind whistled as the trees danced. "How could I return home?" he said, speaking to himself. His beard was growing as the aqua-blue water brushed his broken boat closer. He had an idea... He took his axe to the mysterious forest and got wood. As he returned to the beach after hours and hours, he finally rebuilt his boat. He set sail as the wind took off at speed and he would take what was his...

Ellis Andrews (11)
Greensward Academy, Hockley

The Great Plan!

In the distance, there was a noble Greek living in a mountainous castle. His name was... Alfie the Great. He was as brave as a lion, as strong as a god and he was unbeaten. Alfie the Great was planning an invasion. "Who should we invade next?" he asked.

"The Spartans!" shouted Alfie's loyal soldier Harry. There was a noise. There was a secret Spartan in his castle listening to every word he said. Then there was a bang and a loud thud...

Harrison Vaughan (11)
Greensward Academy, Hockley

The Attack Of The King

A long time ago, Deku was by the king's side when this mysterious man entered the throne room. Deku asked, "Who are you and what do you want?" The man replied, "I'm here to kill the king!" in a mischievous tone.

As soon as the man stopped talking, Deku appeared right up in the man's face and he punched him in the rib. The man then said, "I'm sorry that I didn't introduce myself properly!"

Jack Collier (11)
Greensward Academy, Hockley

Unworthy Punishment

"Ow!" I was thrown into prison. Why? They said treason but I was innocent. Quickly I looked around my cell. It was gloomy and there was mould in every corner. Suddenly, the jailers came in and said, "You unpatriotic moron! Stop plotting against our lovely king! Now your time is up, follow us!" I followed them to a room. There was only one thing in the room: a noose...

Elijah Conway (11)
Greensward Academy, Hockley

A New Land

After one week of sailing, Christopher Columbus and his crew were tired of being on this colossal boat. Then, all of a sudden, Christopher found something in the distance. Immediately, Columbus made the boat go faster and they eventually got to this new land. Columbus and his crew got off the boat and went to the top of the hill. They had discovered America!

Max Raymen (11)
Greensward Academy, Hockley

The Treasure Hunt

A Viking called Erik set up his ship to find the buried treasure. However, there was a problem, there were other Vikings after it! *Kaboom!* A bomb destroyed one of the enemy's ships. Just as Erik and his Vikings got close, another ship approached. Who would get to shore first? Erik bravely shot a bomb and it exploded the other ship just in time!

Henry Waring (11)
Greensward Academy, Hockley

The Chase

The villager sprinted out of the palace, holding onto a map for dear life as the pharaoh and guards chased him. As he ran around the corner, he hid behind a large rock tricking the guards to run past. Zeeka ran rapidly over to the River Nile. He had to swim away and fast...

Lainey Williams (11)
Greensward Academy, Hockley

The Escape

Boom! Suddenly, the ground started to rumble. I stared and saw Mount Vesuvius erupting so I looked down. People were swarming around, looking for safety. Me and my family joined the crowd and screamed, "Run!" We all ran as fast as falcons. My nan took the wrong choice. I tried to look back but my mum tugged me away to Rome. Flames and magma covered Pompeii. Old people in the town were about to meet their fate. Some emperor sisters and brothers were there too. It was too late for grandma. She was encased in ash. "No!" I screamed.

Olena Samantilleke (8)
Hammond Academy, Hemel Hempstead

An Eruption The Size Of A Town

Boom! In the blink of an eye, lava blasted out of Mount Vesuvius. I joined the crowd of petrified residents running towards boats.

When we finally reached the dock, I attempted to jump onto a boat and missed by a tiny inch. After what felt like days, I rested in a wooden boat. I sailed through the rapid sea. It seemed endless. Looking back at Pompeii, all I could see were stones falling upon a frozen-in-time wasteland. With merely a slither of bread, I only took one slice, with the hope of finding civilisation keeping me alive.

Tobias Payne (8)
Hammond Academy, Hemel Hempstead

The End Of Pompeii

Boom! Before I could feel the lava rushing under my feet, I could see a cloud of ash spitting out volcanic lightning. The cloud was triggering lava out of the volcano. The day turned black and people were fighting for safety. Pompeii was about to meet its fate. Everyone was screaming.

I shouted as loud as possible. I said, "This is your one chance to live!"

I was short of breath and smoke infested the sky. I decided to hide. I ran as fast as I could to the random house. I saw I was about to meet my fate...

Dia Gutu (7)
Hammond Academy, Hemel Hempstead

The Volcano Opens Up

Boom! Before I could blink, the ground started rattling. The vast volcano erupted. The houses were shaking. It was boiling. Pompeii was in trouble... big trouble. Pompeii was about to meet its fate. Houses were covered in molten rock. All I could hear were screams bouncing off the walls. I could not feel my body. Feet were stepping on the ground. I couldn't believe the volcano erupted today. These are probably to be my last words. Kids screamed, lava gushed out of the volcano...

Maisie Ward (7)
Hammond Academy, Hemel Hempstead

You Can Never Go

Kaboom! Suddenly, lava spilt out of the volcano. It never stopped spilling out. Ash was flying like birds. People got frozen in time because of the ash. People were running as fast as a train. Houses were damaged. Ash, the colour of burnt coal, was falling on people's heads. People died because they had breathed in fire. People were holding torches. Houses were burnt. Eventually, the lava stopped. Some people survived and some died.

Zayef Mohammed (8)
Hammond Academy, Hemel Hempstead

Grace OH

Curing The Curse

The biting sand swirled towards them. Grace and Bryn fought through it. They thought that they were nearly there.

After hours of walking, Bryn shouted, "We've arrived at Tutankhamun's ancient tomb!"

It was at that moment they remembered the curse.

"We've got the curse!" yelled Grace.

Bryn said, "Time to cure the mysterious curse!"

"Answer this riddle to cure the curse. What is always in front of you but you can't see it?" boomed a strange voice.

"The future," exclaimed Bryn.

"Correct! You no longer have the curse," said the strange voice.

"Who could it be?" Grace wondered.

"Tutankhamun?"

Grace Earl (8)
Harewood Junior School, Tuffley

The Falling Temple

A long time ago, Flower was playing with her friends when she saw a falling temple. They all went to the falling temple. They tried to find things to put it back together. They couldn't find anything. They had a rest then they got back to work. They looked everywhere but they found nothing. One of Flower's friends saw something. All of them went to see what it was.

"It is a man!" said Flower.

"Would you help us?" Flower's friends asked.

The man helped. The man had rocks. They put the temple back together. It took a long time.

Giulia Mitran (8)
Harewood Junior School, Tuffley

Just A Dream?

One day, Daisy woke up. She didn't know where she was, or where Charlie was. She noticed she was in the Valley of the Kings.
"How did I get here?" Daisy said.
Daisy immediately went searching for Charlie. After an hour, there was no luck. Suddenly, coming towards her was something wrapped in toilet paper. As it got closer, she realised it was a mummy. It started storming towards her. Daisy was worried for her life. She fell backwards and fell down, down, down...
When she came round, Charlie was licking her face. It was all just a dream!

Ruby Curran (7)
Harewood Junior School, Tuffley

omg
!

fact
Ruby is friends with charlie and charlie has a sister (or dog) called Daisy!

84

Ancient Egypt

My name is Lily. I live in Egpyt. One day, I was making sandcastles with sand and water. Suddenly, the ground shook for a moment. Then it went as silent as a statue. Suddenly, a person walked up to me and said something in a different language. I didn't understand. I think he said, "Come."
I went with him. I was spooked out at first but it got better. Then something magical happened. I saw something eye-catching. It was beautiful. I saw Tutankhamun's mask. It was unbelievable and mind-blowing. I ran fast to see where I was.

Grace Harris (9)
Harewood Junior School, Tuffley

85

Lost In The Pyramids

One day, a girl called Lilly was in Egypt. She went to the Pyramids of Giza. It was so tall that she had to look so high up. Then she saw something. It was so crazy. It was Tutankhamun. She ran away but got lost in the Pyramids of Giza.
She said, "I'm lost. Oh no! I have an idea."
She went out. She saw a boy. She said, "I can't believe it! Hi, I'm Lilly."
"I'm Jake. Nice to meet you."
They lived happily ever after.

BellaMia Unett (7)
Harewood Junior School, Tuffley

86

Discovery Of A Curse

There was a pharaoh named Bella. She had been a pharaoh for about three years. Bella went for a walk. Suddenly, she tripped on a rock. She sat down for a bit. When she got up, she looked at her ankle because it hurt. Then she burst into tears. It was so bruised.

She managed to get home. When she got home, she lay in bed. She thought, *I was near a tomb, maybe it was a curse to make me trip over and hurt myself?* She decided to never go back to the tomb again.

Ella Bennett (9)
Harewood Junior School, Tuffley

The Egyptian Monster

One dark night, when the guards weren't looking, Arrack and his friends quietly, naughtily and full of hope, snuck into the pyramid of Giza. They had to complete a series of challenges to earn the Staff of Hours which was guarded by an evil pharaoh. Lilly and James crawled silently to the monster and pushed it into a black hole. Arrack grabbed the staff and the friends happily skipped home, overjoyed and feeling like they had the power of the world in their hands.

Jacob James Chambers (7)
Harewood Junior School, Tuffley

he in Lilly (lilly lob)
and James!
my
class Jacob s
Bestles

Elsie? She in my class

Elsie And Her Grandad's Tomb

It was just a normal day at Elsie's school. She was thinking about her grandad. All of a sudden, Elsie teleported to her grandad's tomb. She thought, *I wonder what happened to Grandad before he died?* She was thinking and thinking. She thought maybe he had a curse on him. All of a sudden, she saw her grandad. She was so glad to see him. A couple of days after, she was very sick. She thought it could be the curse...

Beatrice Long (8)
Harewood Junior School, Tuffley

A Pharoah's Medicine

One day, Kire visited a pharaoh. The pharaoh was sick. Kire went to his house and made a medicine but her cat destroyed it. It drank it and vanished. Kire made a new one. Suddenly, Kire started being chased by scorpions. He teleported and ran but they went in front of him. Suddenly, his cat hit the scorpions. Kire ran as quickly as he could to give the pharaoh the medicine. The pharaoh gulped it and said, "Thank you!"

Kian Baker (8)
Harewood Junior School, Tuffley

The Curse

Suddenly, Chris woke up in the middle of nowhere. There was sand everywhere. He saw something sticking out of the sand. It was a mask. He ran to it but then he saw someone running towards him. He ran as fast as he could and fell. The man came to him. The man said that Chris had to solve a curse. The curse was that he had to find Tutankhamun because he was sick and he had to make him better.

Lily Cole (9)
Harewood Junior School, Tuffley

Woolly Makes New Friends

Once upon a time, there was a big bad T-rex, his name was Zacum. He had a nice friend, Zac, and they went on an adventure. They went to look for treasure that was 10,000 old. It was buried by Jon Depp, next to the washed-up ship, Pirates Battle. It took them 5 years to reach the ship, but they did not know that Woolly, the woolly mammoth was hiding onboard!

Woolly jumped out and begged them to be his friend, because he was the last mammoth alive. He was lonely.

The three became friends and went on adventures together!

Nico Gillies/McGarrell (8)
Kennoway Primary School, Kennoway

Theseus And The Sea Monster

Many days ago, there lived a powerful and mighty man called Theseus. He had a very deep voice and was built like a wrestler. He was as strong as a boar. This is the place where the sea monster lived. The sea monster worked with Medusa and they were planning to kill Theseus and Hermione. The cave was full of shadows and piercing screams. Hermione was a sweet princess chained to a rock that is about to collapse. Theseus said, "Oh no, are you okay? What happened?"
Hermione said, "Please help me I'm stuck to a rock..."

Hollie Brayshaw (9)
Killamarsh Junior School, Killamarsh

Ajax And Clio

In a land of heroes and gods lived Ajax. He was brave and as fast as a cheetah.

Clio met a scaly monster with three red eyes. It was evil and chained the petrified Clio to the slimy rocks. Terrified, Clio trembled, waiting for the evil monster to attack her.

Ajax flew to Clio's defence to slay the wicked gorgon.

Jack Davis (8)
Killamarsh Junior School, Killamarsh

Mammoths

I awoke to an immense sound. It was like a walking earthquake, drowning all other noises as it passed. "Mammoths!" The cry echoed through our cave, yet it was still barely audible. I took up my newly-made spear, eager to join the hunt. Their shadow turned our patch of snowfield to darkness as we rushed out of the mountainside shrieking and cheering. We were battered and bruised, but still we persisted. And despite the mammoths' crushing force, they fell. That night, we feasted on mammoth meat, amongst songs and cheers and roars of laughter.

Alice Bain (11)
Marden High School, North Shields

The Magic Rod

One really good afternoon Stig grabbed 100 berries and then saw a stand. He went to see it quickly.

Stig said, "What are the cheapest things here?"

"A fishing rod," the man said.

"I'll have that please," said Stig.

Then Stig went fishing for a second, and then Stig went to a different universe! All he did was catch ten fish. Now it was winter. So he caught ten more but it didn't work. So he caught twenty more and it worked. It was summer again.

Sami Goolfee (8)
Maylandsea Primary School, Maylandsea

A Land Far Away

Once upon a time, in a land far away there was a dragon. However, this wasn't any old dragon, this was a wood dragon. The thing about wood dragons is that they love the forest. They love to make new trees everywhere they go, make flowers blossom and most of all they love the rain.
One hot summer's day, the wood dragon heard a loud noise, it sounded like a tree being cut down. Although the wood dragon didn't mind people he hated anything that killed or hurt nature so he rushed to the noise and saw another wood dragon...

Caleb West (11)
Millbank Academy, London

The Hating Mummy

Clouds of sand blow across the desert. Inside a pyramid a group of tourists are searching for mummies. Suddenly, a tall beige mummy leaps out and shouts, "Get out!"
The tourists scream, but one of them says, "No need to be so rude, learn to love instead."
The mummy says, "Shut your face," but the tourist doesn't leave.
"I will not leave until you learn to love."
The mummy says, "I never thought of that, but I will try it later."
The tourist nods their head and smiles. Later on, the mummy tries and they feel happy.
Learn to love.

Abigail Appleton (6)
Milton Parochial Primary School, Milton Malsor

Shark And The Boys

One eye opened, two eyes opened... Two boys were floating in a boat in the ocean. All of a sudden, the boat tipped over. *Splash!* "Ouch!" One boy saw some Egyptian men building a pyramid on land. "How are we back in time?"
"I don't know!"
"Quick, swim!"
They both swam for their lives. But one boy saw a shark. "Shark!"
The other boy said, "Swim!"
The shark chased the boys. One boy did not make it. The shark took one bite and swallowed. "Nooo!" The other boy was almost alive but then one mouth opened and then, *chomp!*

Alexia Herberts (9)
Newton On Trent CE Primary School, Newton On Trent

The Labyrinth

Many, many years ago, there lived a famous Greek hero named Ernie Blackshadow. He became a hero in 440 BC for defeating the horrible, dreaded beast named the Deathpanther. It was a pet that belonged to King Radius and only ate human flesh! Radius forced people into the labyrinth where the monstrous creature dwelled and left them to die there. One day, Ernie volunteered to go into the labyrinth where he found it and returned from the labyrinth with its head in his arms.

Since then, he's been known as a legendary hero in Greek mythology and still is now.

Kai Tsui (10)
Our Lady Of Lourdes Catholic Primary School, Finchley

ANCIENT ADVENTURES 2022 - ASTONISHING ADVENTURES

The Time Machine

Below the dense forest, swaying trees stood tall and proud. Over the wavy grass a metal head was protruding out. The colossal machine was half-hidden by a blanket of crisp-like leaves. Not long after, an explorer called Bob stumbled across a new find. Bob got out his trusty pickaxe and started digging. Suddenly, *whoosh*. He vanished into thin air. Bob found himself at the battle of Watling Street. Bob could see, grassy plains and massive hills. Bob felt his blood run cold. He was frozen with fear. Bob tried to think of a way to get out of this place...

Michele Zeolla (9)
Our Lady Of Lourdes Catholic Primary School, Finchley

The Battle Of The Biggest Wars With A Twist

My family and I went to the history museum to look at wars, we went to the middle.

We took a peek at the Romans' exhibition and saw emperor Nero battling the Egyptian leader. Boudicca and the Egyptians burned Rome and killed Nero.

We were surprised. We wandered off to World War I and saw the whole world teaming up on Bulgaria and it went up in flames then they aimed for Africa but Africa was too powerful so destroyed the coming country China. We were hoping World War II was not real but it was and we nearly died...

Derek Ayeni (9)
Our Lady Of Lourdes Catholic Primary School, Finchley

Attack Of Gozorpozorp

Once upon a time, lived a mighty, vicious and beastly knight in a minuscule village. He was on a mission, a once-in-a-lifetime mission, to save the universe. So he packed his mighty sword and shield and then set off on his mission. He travelled far and wide to the ends of the earth then he finally came across his destination. "Hello Gozorpozorp," said the mighty knight.
"We finally meet again," said Gozorpozorp.
They fought hours and hours ongoing. But finally, there was only one remaining standing incredibly strong. But there it was, standing in front of him...

Jude Skates (9)
Parklands Primary School, Northampton

The Locked Door

Once upon a time, there was a little girl called Lily. She was sleeping one night and she heard rattling from the wardrobe. She opened it and saw a mummy. She screamed. She ran downstairs to the bathroom and locked it. The mummy was trying to get in but he could not. She was panicking.
The mummy finally unlocked the door.
Backtracking to the wall, Lily shouted for help and the mummy started crying because he didn't mean to scare the girl. They became friends, best of friends, and the mummy was kind after all.

Kacey Collins (8)
Parklands Primary School, Northampton

The Murder Of A Dragon

123 years ago, Professor Smirling created the mythical creature of a dragon. As soon as it woke up he killed the professor and escaped the lab. He went to the town of Darkita. It destroyed the houses, shops and hospitals.

A boy called Charlie was fed up of this so he went to the attic and got armour and a ride to kill the dragon. Charlie climbed up the mountain and all he saw was a dragon roaring at him, ready to breathe out fire. Charlie then looked the dragon in the eyes and killed the beast with cold lead...

Theo Underwood (10)
Parklands Primary School, Northampton

The Viking And His Gem

Once, a homeless Viking went on an adventure. He was walking for miles to find a gem. Unfortunately, it wasn't a normal adventure. It was a scary one. He was walking up the hills, looking super excited, but when he got to the top he was greeted by a mummy, a scary mummy. He knew he had to defeat it, to kill it. So he did. He pulled off its power, its paper. Just like that, it had turned to stone. He had done it. He quickly grabbed the gem and was able to afford a nice, cosy cave.

Elsie Roberts (10)
Parklands Primary School, Northampton

Time Travel

One day in ancient Egypt, Akhenaten was enjoying his banquet with Nefertiti. The one person who really hated him was Anya. Tutankhamun was the next pharaoh and how she prayed Akhenaten would die. Luckily, she had a time travel clock. she just didn't know what pharaoh would get it. Anya had a brilliant idea. She grabbed her dad's wrist. They went to the old kingdom. her dad's jaw dropped.

"Well," said Anya. "Let's live our lives!"

Her dad was very confused. When he looked back she was gone so he decided to run after her.

Anya Barrett-Prior (8)
Place Farm Primary Academy, Haverhill

King Tut

It was a scorching hot day in the middle of the Egyptian desert. I was on a mission to find the tomb of Tutankhamun.

When I found the tomb, I had to solve a puzzle. When I made it inside the tomb, I made a magnificent discovery. It gave me goosebumps. The whole tomb was made of gold. As I stood inside the tomb, I stepped on a booby trap. The room started to fill with sand. I had to escape quickly.

When I got home, no one believed the story of my adventure.

Poppy Wheeler (8)
Place Farm Primary Academy, Haverhill

World War II

World War II: Steve Jefferson awoke with a gun on his desk. He soon finally realised that everyone was standing in front of him with all their equipment ready to fight. Steve and all the other soldiers set off to Europe with guns, grenades, knives and other types of weapons in their bags. Once they had landed, they left the flying vehicle and entered the war zone. They went to their big den to get ready for the war. Steve was sick and they had to finish it next year. Steve returned unharmed.

Bleu Cass (9)
Ruislip Gardens Primary School, Ruislip

The Pacific Adventure

Hey, let me tell you a story. It starts in the Pacific. There was a boy called Jake. Jake was 19 years old, his dad died when he was 9. He had built a ship called the great Titanic. On the way to America, there was a tremble and giant iceberg rose up. The ship couldn't stop! It was about to crash and Jake realised it and dived to see what was happening. There was a hole. Before he could report it, the ship was sinking. He was too late!

Arjun Shankar (8)
Ruislip Gardens Primary School, Ruislip

Break Out Blackness

I was sent to the workhouse. Pulled from my family. I needed to escape. The machines clattered, clashed and crashed loudly. I needed help. A child came to me asking for help. He wanted to escape too. "We should escape at nightfall!" I suggested.
"What about Matron?"
"Who cares," I said whispering very quietly.
"Okay, but I still don't know about this," he said.
"At lights out meet here."
I left him alone. We met back up at lights out. We grabbed the key from the sleeping Matron and ran. She chased us. I ran until blackness hit me...

Ashton Phillips (10)
Shade Primary School, Shade

Queen Elizabeth Is Trapped!

Trapped! I'm trapped in a tower, hardly enough food to last a day. Will I die of thirst in this scorching hot weather or will I be forgotten about? But I have a plan! "I will escape," I shout at the top of my lungs. "Bye Tower of London, hello freedom." I knock down the door with my long, heavy robe on. I run, sneaking down, but I've gone wrong. I'm being chased. Running down the road like it's a maze, I find a place to hide. Beneath the officer's desk is decent... right? I'll be back. Trapped! "Help me..."

Laila Harris (10)
Shade Primary School, Shade

Factory Escape

On a bitterly cold winter night, fires lit up every house. It was a stormy night and everything was silent apart from the clanging of factory machines followed by the screams of children. There was a boy called Gregory who had a friend called Ted. They were planning to escape and were talking about it. They took a minecart and dragged it outside but sadly they were caught and left the minecart outside but that was the whole idea of their plan. They climbed through the vents to escape outside and they went down a dark alleyway...

Sam Knowles (10)
Shade Primary School, Shade

A Temple Break-In

The sand burnt my feet; whilst the sun hit my face. One scorching night in ancient Greece something totally unexpectant happened! Last night someone broke in. We didn't know what to do and what they stole until we checked the basement... They stole all our gold! We needed to find out who stole it and need to get it back! "I've got a plan! He must still be in the building because we have guards so someone dresses up as a mummy and he'll touch other things and we will scare him."
"Good idea!"

Emily Smith (9)
Shade Primary School, Shade

The Prisoner

The queen was gone. The Germans took her. They ruled England. I was enslaved, they were rough, they'd bombed us. I was her guard. I'd been gagged. How would we regain England? I had shackles on my legs, then I saw a key. I just grabbed it. I was free. After knocking a guard unconscious, I stole his uniform and key and went to the bomb shelter where the queen was. I went to the door but alarms were ringing. I heard many steps. I was trapped. I was about to escape but then it all went black.

Joseph Hardcastle (10)
Shade Primary School, Shade

The Revealing Of Cleopatra

In Egypt on a hot day, the scorching desert was exhausting. The Egyptians were working very hard wrapping up mummies. "I am the pharaoh," Cleopatra would say. She was the only pharaoh. The sand burnt through my feet. I didn't know what to do, I didn't know what to say. "My dad died recently so I am the queen." I entered the pyramid. There were so many artefacts from before I was born. I heard big footsteps coming towards me. I blinked but all I could see was darkness...

Alice Williams (9)
Shade Primary School, Shade

The Philosopher

A long time ago, in ancient Greece far away, a Greek philosopher (Gyro) had set off on a journey. He had gone to a desert to find a new medicine. He set off on his journey to find the magic. He wandered the desert to find something, but nothing. He began to get hungry so he looked for some food. He found some bread his wife had made for him. Suddenly, a snake approached him. Without warning, the snake went up to Gyro and bit him! He lay on the ground and died horribly just wanting to go home.

Aoife Brown (10)
Shade Primary School, Shade

Escape From The Mills

We have been in this wretched, disgusting place for days, weeks, years even. We all wanted to get out. We had to but how could we? It was obvious, we could steal the key on the master's waist. I went up and carefully grabbed the key. When it was night-time we carefully crept out of bed. As we got to the bottom of the stairs we heard footsteps so we hid under the tables. One of the children jumped out and screamed. The rest of us ran as fast as possible. We were finally now outside.

Rhudi Warren (10)
Shade Primary School, Shade

World War II

In 1940 England went to war with Germany, it was a wet day when I got chosen to go to war. I was scared thinking I'd never return. We were heading to London for the first battle. Over sixty people died but I survived. On the third to last war nearly eighteen million people were dead. We were on our last part of the war, it was gruesome. I was so scared to go to this one. I was so scared I fainted. I remember that day until I was rushed to the doctor and died.

Evan Bonny (10)
Shade Primary School, Shade

The Mummy

My friends went to ancient Egypt. There was lots of sand and a pyramid nearby. They saw something move very fast. They went to see what it was. The pyramid door shut and they were trapped. I went to find my friends. I was scared as they had been missing for a week. I saw a weird temple but it was shut. I wondered if they were in there so I tried to find a way to get in. I was in, there were traps all the way. A mummy was alive, I ran!

Casper Hird (10)
Shade Primary School, Shade

Doctor Time

I stepped down on the wet cobbled road. I had rewound all of time and I was searching the gruesome Victorian streets for the people of the future and past. Suddenly, I saw Alfred and zapped him with my watch and I sent him back to his era. I then repeated the operation that would have everyone sent to their own era. I ran to my time machine and everything went back to normal except there is still one future man out there...

Henry Gulaiczuk (10)
Shade Primary School, Shade

The 'Normal' School Day

It was another horrible Monday. I had a whole week at school so I got up and dressed. Soon I was dressed and went to school. When I got there I was too late to wash my hands and I couldn't ask because I would get hit! I then saw the teacher and he was coming towards me. My hands were struck by the cane. I was the worst pupil in the whole school. I went home, sat down and cried.

Joseph Connor (10)
Shade Primary School, Shade

Ares The Spartan Warrior

My name is Ares. I was named after the god of war. It's 405 BC and we are fighting against the Athenian army. We have been fighting for over twenty-nine years now. I was born during the war. Now, I'm hiding beside my friend's dead bodies in a temple. Suddenly, I get attacked by two Athenians. I either run or fight back. I decide to fight them. Determined, I viciously fight the terrifying over-optimistic Athenians that are considerably older than me.

Eventually, I won the war in 404 BC. The Spartan army can never be beaten.

Nelly Dymecka (9)

St Augustine Webster Catholic Primary School, Scunthorpe

The Anglo-Saxon

Exhausted, Viki the Anglo-Saxon warrior was fighting the Vikings for two days straight in 793 AD. Unfortunately, her village burned down to the ground. She had an idea, she would collect pieces of wood from her village and take it to a place far away from the Vikings. After a week, she made herself a village for her future family. She also took some seeds to plant but she only had wheat and barley. "I am happy in my village. I am so glad I did not die because I wouldn't live a happy life like this."

Victoria Skrzyszowska (10)
St Augustine Webster Catholic Primary School, Scunthorpe

The Ancient Last Princess

1005 years ago, a girl called Raya was watering the crops. All of a sudden, a flood happened. After the flood. she thought about where she came from. Suddenly, Tutankhamun spoke to Raya and said she was his daughter. She didn't believe him. Then she realised she was wearing an Egyptian dress and realised she was Tutankhamun's daughter. Then a mummy chased her until she tripped. Blood was everywhere. She washed it in the River Nile. After, she looked at the sky. Her mum and dad were happily there. They lived happily.

Martha Houlton (8)
St Catherine's CE Primary School, Launceston

The Great Escape

Belle was cleaning up the workhouse like a regular evening when, all of a sudden, there was a smash! An expensive vase had fallen. An enormous tsunami of sorrow flooded her mind and there was a *thump! Thump! Thump!* She knew she would be punished and beaten. She'd already lost a finger from sleeping in five minutes. But this was worse! Would she lose all of them? Then she noticed a window open. This was the only way she could get out of there. With a crash, she was out. Suddenly, she heard even louder footsteps than before...

Kaitlen Horan (9)
St Francis Primary School, Bradford

The Great Fire Of London

One day, in a bakery, a baker was baking a cake. Then the baker had to leave the room. Suddenly the fire inside the oven got bigger and bigger. After some time, the entire bakery was on fire! All the people ran for their lives. The fire ran around the town like a lightning bolt. After some time, the fire was now spreading faster through London. Then the flaming fire with the colours red, orange and yellow got stronger and stronger. The fire invaded the town. It spread as fast as a cheetah. What could they do now...?

George Illingworth (8)
St Francis Primary School, Bradford

The Unexpected Place

One boiling day, a mummy called Mimi was in a weird place. "Where am I?" Mimi said to herself. From the corner of her eye, she saw a Viking. "Hey?" she shouted.

The Viking turned around. He said to Mimi that he could find a way out. When they walked for hours in the place, they arrived at a portal. It teleported to where they came from.

Soon after, Mimi went back to have a rest, a long rest. It lasted ages since she was a mummy. We hope that nothing like this ever happens again to Mimi.

Sraiyah Williams (10)
St James' CE Primary School, Oldbury

The Robot

Once, in the past, a person had a robot that cleaned everything in the house but the person actually set it up wrong and soon it had a sword and a backpack with an electric thing and the robot was soon cleaning the whole place and then it was trying to kill everyone! The owner of the robot tried to do the puzzle to disarm it. He did it! When he hit the button, he fell out of the window. He was okay though and went back to cleaning the house.

San Aula (9)
St Joseph's Primary School, Gabalfa

The Discovery

Howard Carter entered Tutankhamun's tomb. He slowly removed his mask from Tutankhamun's face. Howard took a few steps back once he removed the mask because of all the mould growing on his face and body.

After discovering Tutankhamun's tomb they found many items and gold. Then before doing anything with the body, they cleaned and re-embalmed the body. They cleaned the jars containing Tutankhamun's liver, heart, lungs, brain and stomach.

They flew his sarcophagus to London and placed it in a popular museum and now anyone around the world can visit Tutankhamun's sarcophagus.

Zarah Bernard (10)
St Luke's Catholic Primary School, Trench

Great Fire Of London

Suddenly, a spark flew up in the air and caught onto a wooden brush and then that caught on fire the half-covered house. It spread from house to house. The screams got louder and louder as more houses went up in flames. The firefighters tried to stop the fire but they couldn't, the fire was too big. Everyone evacuated their houses, grabbing everything they could if it wasn't on fire. Loads of people died. It stopped because that day it rained and when the fire stopped everyone was happy and grateful.

Joseph Hogan (10)
St Margaret's CE Primary School, Horsforth

Jackson And The Ferocious Vikings

Jackson had a glittering time machine that he could travel in time with. Suddenly, the time machine sucked him up and malfunctioned.

He woke up in Viking Britain, as he heard swords and shields clashing together. Without a doubt, he wasn't being careful, he sprinted and hit a window and the last thing he saw was a man in a grey helmet getting stabbed with an axe, not making it out alive. But then the time machine came back and took a Viking with it...

Ethan Knight (9)
St Margaret's CE Primary School, Horsforth

My Great Gran

Let's start. This is a story about my great-grandma, she was in the Great Fire of London. She was a firefighter and saved lots of lives, 100 lives to be exact. She was a hero to people and she is a hero to me, she even died a hero. She died saving a disabled girl called Mia, who could not walk or talk. Gran nearly survived but breathed in too much smoke from the fire. If it was not for my great-gran, lots more people would have died.

Nancy Callaghan (10)
St Margaret's CE Primary School, Horsforth

Hades Vs Zeus

Hello, my name is Zeus. It was a normal day before Hades took over. He broke the colosseum and destroyed the land with frogs, we had to stop him.
"Come on, Hades is on Olympus, I didn't know how but..."
"Woah, he sees us run, run! Argh!"
"I'll zap him!"
Zap! Zap!
"Hey, shoot him with your fire!"
Blast!
"Hey, we got him!"
"Thanks for your help. I've got a gift for you, here your own lightning gun, just like Thor's hammer and thunderclouds."
"See you soon, bye-bye."

Paul Mcardle (8)
St Margaret's Primary Academy, Lowestoft

Vikings

Suddenly, I placed my hand onto the cool rock and looked up. On the snowy mountains there were piles of glaciers. Beneath me, there was a ton of menacing volcanoes. I hoped I would make it to safety. I desperately needed some sky iron, that's why I was climbing up a vast cliff.

If you didn't already know, I'm Abbie and I'm a girl Viking. I really needed some more metal for armour and shields for my husband so he could go to battle. I'm normally raiding and trading, so I don't know why he sent me to do this...

Abbie Attew (10)
St Margaret's Primary Academy, Lowestoft

Mr Blue Bob

Mr Blue Bob was a small blob of blue gelatinous material. Although he had a kind appearance, he was a master thief! He was able to steal the king's crown, leaving no trace at all.

One misty day, Mr Blue Bob decided he wanted to steal the diamond skull. While nobody was looking, he slid his way through a crack in the ancient pyramid. He swiftly made his way through, dodging all the pitfalls, spike launchers and rolling boulders. Finally, he came to a stop and quickly snatched the skull. As quick as a flash, he disappeared.

Jacob Bale (11)
St Margaret's Primary Academy, Lowestoft

The Ancient Greeks

Olivia was a 16-year-old girl who loved history. One day, she and her friends decided to go to the history museum. As they were walking through, Olivia and her friends noticed the ancient Greek section. They walked in and went over to some pottery, Olivia touched a piece of pottery and strangely she felt a sharp shock. She was in ancient Greek times! In shock, Olivia wandered around, suddenly she was being chased. She ran and ran, and found that same piece of pottery she had touched before. She touched it again and was home.

Mila Lubbock (10)
St Margaret's Primary Academy, Lowestoft

The Memosaurus

It's the Jurassic era and the memosaurus is on it again, slaughtering everything in its path with its power to create earth and land anywhere, dropping rocks on other forms of life and letting nothing stop it. It had already taken one quarter of the dinosaurs, it was an apex predator. But something was wrong, there was not another dinosaur in sight. Little did it know, right behind it were all the dinosaurs. They jumped on his back and all attacked it and it was done, it was dead. Finally they were safe and ran around in joy.

Joseph Knight (10)
St Margaret's Primary Academy, Lowestoft

The Vicious Viking

Dalton was going on a school trip with his school. When they arrived at the museum, they had a really good look around the old dinosaur skeletons and then something interesting caught Dalton's eyes. He saw a red button. He pressed it and felt his body tingle. Then he was suddenly in the Vikings' age, he was in the past! Suddenly, he was chased by a Viking, then there were multiple Vikings! He ran faster and faster, then faster, then all of a sudden he was back on his coach. His teacher told him off badly.

Dalton Welton (11)
St Margaret's Primary Academy, Lowestoft

A New Stone Age

It's cold and dark, the rain has come through the roof, the roof can't hold the rain out. We're wet, it is dark and the nights are long. My father is strong, he's hunting for food to keep us alive, let's hope he can survive. My brother is brave, he looks after us all, he helps keep us alive. My mum is scared... it's too late, he must be gone... My father is dead and everyone is sad. We have no food and are scared we will not live. We cannot survive, we are not safe. No one can help...

Zoe Morris (8)
St Margaret's Primary Academy, Lowestoft

140

Living With Dinosaurs

One day, there was a girl who loved dinosaurs. She went to look for some, she looked and looked and found a dinosaur, she lived with them. Sadly, they went missing. There was a parrot and he helped her find the dinosaurs, she looked and looked and finally found them. She never let them get lost again. She didn't want to go home so she made a plan, she would take the dinosaurs home. So she did and they were all happy and all lived happily ever after.

Kaitie-Jade Stockley (9)
St Margaret's Primary Academy, Lowestoft

Viking Venus

There was a Viking called Venus and he found a time machine in his house. So he set it to 45 million years ago. He saw a tyrannosaurus rex. The dinosaur kicked up Venus with his teeth and took him to his cave. There he met another tyrannosaurus rex. When the tyrannosaurus rex put him down he had bits of blood on him and massive teeth marks on his head!
Then he time-travelled back to his time.

Lacie Coleman (9)
St Margaret's Primary Academy, Lowestoft

Garfunkle's Adventure

"I'm going to find a dinosaur fossil," said Garfunkle, the woolly mammoth.
So he went on an adventure and eventually he saw a bone, so he started digging and eventually dug up the whole thing! Garfunkle took it home.
He made a time machine to take him back in time. So he typed in a date and it took him back, but the dinosaurs there tried to eat him!

Oscar Cushion (10)
St Margaret's Primary Academy, Lowestoft

Henry VIII

I was sweeping the palace when I stumbled across something. It was Henry VIII. He was looking for a professional artist. I assumed that Henry was looking for a new wife after divorcing the first one. I rolled my eyes. I couldn't help but eavesdrop... Soon, he found another artist, after finding out that he was going to be both the king and the father of a newborn baby girl. He must've disowned the baby because right after she was born, she randomly disappeared...

Eseosa Osayande (11)
St Mark's Catholic Primary School, Great Barr

I Met The Mayans

Yesterday, I was walking to the shops to buy some food. I saw my regular shopkeeper, Raj. He said he didn't work at the shop anymore. He gave me a special drink and told me to drink it in two days then I would see him again.

After two days, I drank it. I could not believe it. I woke up and I was in Mayan times. I found Raj's shop. I found a man who looked like Raj from the back but it wasn't him. I looked everywhere for him but he couldn't be found.

Raiyaana Rehman (10)
St Mark's Catholic Primary School, Great Barr

Boudicca The Brave

Boudicca lived in East Anglia where she led a tribe of Celtic warriors. In AD 60 Boudicca led a revolt against the Romans who had taken all her money, belongings and land. While the Roman army was in Wales Boudicca's army destroyed the Roman towns of St Albans, Colchester and London. The Roman army trapped Boudicca's army and defeated them at the Battle of Watling Street. The Romans then ruled most of Britain for 350 years. Boudicca is remembered as a ferocious warrior. There is a statue of her outside the Houses of Parliament in London.

Imogen Richardson (9)
St Mary's CE Primary School, Sale

Evlin's Evil Pyramid Story

My name is Evil Evlin. I went to a mysterious pyramid for an evil trip. I was so hungry that I started eating the fruit I'd bought. I've killed lots of people because they murdered my whole family. Everyone at the pyramid had said that my family should be massacred so then they were killed. But since then, soldiers have been following me. I am so worried that they will find me.

My real name is Lila but my parents called me Evlin because I was cheeky. I wish my parents were here.

Oh no! They're here...

Aima Waqar (9)
St Michael's CE Primary School, Bolton

I Want To See My Family

I am the youngest soldier in the Roman army. I am so tired. I want to see my family. I haven't seen them for two years. I want to escape. I am so bored and frightened that I might die and not see my family again. I have a plan. I will eat a rotten rat and I will pretend that I am dead and they will throw me in the sea...

I swam across the sea and reached Laspiza. My family weren't there so I went to another country to find them.

Mahnoor Khan (9)
St Michael's CE Primary School, Bolton

Eoster's Story

My hair swished from side to side; my name's Eoster, an Anglo-Saxon god. My job is to rebirth the wonderful spring's nature. I was beautiful.
As I skipped gracefully, I suddenly heard a prayer to me. It said, "Dear Eoster, this year please make our crops grow otherwise my people won't have anything to eat. Please Eoster! From Harriet."
I answered in my soft voice, "Yes Harriet, I will make the sun and rain fall upon your village." The spring bounced up like a bunny, eating a lucky carrot. She did what she was told and they were all happy!

Issacisla Hayman (9)
St Paul's CE Junior School, Kingston Upon Thames

Young Writers

Tutankhamun's Return

As I woke up, I could only see darkness. Where was I? When I tried to remember, my mind was blank. After I had gotten out of this sarcophagus, I wondered what I was doing in there. Suddenly, a group of tourists came in and I told them to leave as I was king, wasn't I? They were just laughing and they said it was 2022. If they weren't going to make me their pharaoh, I would make it on my own. Without warning, a messenger arrived and bowed down at me. Everyone was puzzled. I waited for my coronation...

Talha Ahmad (10)
St Sebastian's RC Primary School, Douglas Green

150

Smugglers

I'm Robin, just a normal fisherman's son from Robin Hood's Bay. The night this story started was a horrible, windy Tuesday. I was sleeping uncomfortably on the floor in our cottage when I woke to the sound of creaking floorboards. As soon as I opened my eyes, I wished I hadn't because there at the bottom of the room, stood a man. Not just any man, a smuggler! The man noticed me. "Hey kid," he said. "What are you looking at?" "Sm-mug-gler!" I stuttered. "Yeah, so now you know who I am, we're gonna take you away..."

Abigail Snodgrass (10)
Starbeck Primary Academy, Starbeck

The Lost Girl And The Hungry Viking

In a long field there was a girl and she was lost, looking for her mother. She came across a house and stood next to the door and then suddenly, "Raa!"

"Oh!" said the girl. "Please, help me find my way home," she pleaded.

"Eh?" said the grumpy Viking. "What's in it for me?" he asked stumbling out of his home.

"I'll give you bread."

"Deal!"

"Follow me then."

They took days to get there but when they did this happened... "Now that you're home give me bread!"

"No way!"

"Huh?"

"Just kidding. Bye Mr!"

Leanna Holl (9)
Temple Mill Primary School, Strood

War Of Britain

Chop! The Saxon's head came off. The Vikings declared war on the Saxons. Someone named Luke was kidnapped, it was misery, Redneck the Viking king. He roamed to Denmark and got 5,000 men and killed 987 people just with 2,000 men and the new Saxon king decided to go behind the Vikings and in front. That made them almost win the war. Meanwhile, Luke was in hell, he had to eat dung. "I almost died eating poo and drinking wee." But the Vikings didn't give up, in fact, they won so they sat round a campfire and celebrated.

Luke Gorham (9)
Temple Mill Primary School, Strood

Naughty Viking Who Turns Into A Good Viking

Our Viking is called Dimple. He is very naughty but he loves his family but Dimple has no friends so no one comes to his parties. Once Dimple was so naughty he stole all the shields before war. 12 people died. People were so mad then Dimple was really sad so he wanted to be nice. He helped old people carry heavy things and if he listened to music he would put the volume down to the minimum so people could sleep and taught himself manners. Now he is so polite and loads of people come to his parties.

Esmai Pook (8)
Temple Mill Primary School, Strood

The War In Britain

Sven was outside one day because it was very hot but as soon as Sven went in his castle Vikings ran past. Sven ran into the castle and warned the others that Vikings were attacking. Sven and the others got their swords, spears and shields and ran charging at the Vikings. Sven stopped the war before anyone else got hurt. Sven chased the Vikings from the castle that night. Sven, Savern and Ven hung decorations and Miger baked the food. "Delicious! This food is sooo good!" they all said.

Poppy Cobb (9)
Temple Mill Primary School, Strood

The Wild West

As we were riding our horses through the dusty sand, we saw a gang of sheriffs standing in front of us. We rode off and cheekily said, "Poop ya later." They tried to shoot us as they'd seen our wanted signs. We were the baddest gang in the west. We're Jesse James, Pika Mix and Decor. One of the sheriffs challenged us to a shootout. We grabbed our pistols. We were nervous. *Could this be the day we die?* We hopped on our white gypsy horses and rode to the bar. Suddenly, the sheriffs kicked down the door. *Bang! Bang!*

Jesse McIntosh (11)

The Bishops' CE Learning Academy, Treninnick Hill

The Tudors

There once was a girl who went out to get bread for her family from a nearby village. The dragon's castle was perched on top of a hill in the shape of a mountain. The girl, Margret, saw the dragon wake up. It flew into sight, right near the village. The fellow citizens of Hermania, the village, were scared because the dragon had just burnt the village's only bakery, just after Margret came out. Margret's friend, Anna the dragon defeater, came and killed the dragon with her sword. The day was over. After that, they heard another dragon...

Summer Crowther (11)
The Bishops' CE Learning Academy, Treninnick Hill

The Black Death

One strange evening that did not feel right at all, all I could see were people dying because of the rats. Rats were carrying diseases from years ago. Unfortunately, the whole town caught it. Devastating news. Everyone in the village died. The rats had taken over the village. In biscuit tins and cupboards, everywhere. The rats were taking over the world until the bacteria started to go. The rats began to slowly die off. The humans figured that out and started coming out of their houses. They went down the pub to celebrate.

Stanley Richardson (11)
The Bishops' CE Learning Academy, Treninnick Hill

Romans - The War Against The Invaders

I had woken up to a perfect morning. I went outside to see my friends. They were hanging out by the fountain. It was quiet outside. When we were bored, everyone was awake. Suddenly, our Roman leader was shouting that there were invaders coming. I was already a soldier, so our leader gave me a weapon and sent me to the others. Me and my team were sent onto the battleground. We all ran towards the invaders. I went and killed four but got injured. That's when I decided I would run. So I ran. But someone chased me. Oh...

Samuel Rawsthorn (11)

The Bishops' CE Learning Academy, Treninnick Hill

The Black Death

The midnight sky beamed on the city of London like a million flashlights. The rats came out of the sewers and drains carrying a deadly disease, but nobody knew. Darkness. It was dark in my eyes. I awoke, trapped. I was trapped underground in a box. My eyes widened; I tried to scream for help but nothing came out. Scared. I was scared. It was pitch-black. I shut my eyes to calm down. Spoiler alert: I never woke up. Was it all a dream? Please let me live, I'm only ten. Just like that, death. Rats. *Boom! Boom!*

Miley Hill (10)
The Bishops' CE Learning Academy, Treninnick Hill

Ancient Egypt

On a dark, rainy day, Millie was outside. She found a shed. She went inside and fell into a dark tunnel which went deep down.

A while later, Millie landed in a desert. She saw the pyramid of Giza. Millie entered the pyramid. She found a key on the ground. Millie kept walking.

A while later, she found another key. Millie was scared. She found a door, unlocked it and in the room, she found a tomb. She used the other key. She unlocked the tomb and then she saw a time machine. She went inside... She was home.

Maja Abram (10)
The Bishops' CE Learning Academy, Treninnick Hill

Dinosaurs

When the sun rose into the pink and yellow forever lasting sky, I woke up and was hungry. So I went hunting in the deep, light green forest. It was really dark but I could still see. Suddenly, I decided I wanted to eat a brachiosaurus. At the end of the forest, there was a herd of brachiosauruses. They didn't see me, so I went on the attack. I caught one. All of a sudden, I saw something fall out of the sky. Darkness fell...

Izak Lategan (10)
The Bishops' CE Learning Academy, Treninnick Hill

The Mummy

Once upon a time, there was a mummy. She always wanted to fulfil her dreams but bad things happened to her. She always wanted to be an engineer but at that time she was in high school. Everybody said, "You are a girl, you can never be an engineer." Other people made fun of her bandages wrapped over her.
She concentrated on her future so she studied cars and eventually she became a civil engineer. They had a mummy party and everyone wore bandages.

Fatimah Khan (9)
The Godolphin Junior Academy, Slough

The Water Mystery

One day in the desert, there was pharaoh who wanted water. He went to the river but there was no water. He called his servant. His servant went and got a pipe fixer.

The pipe fixer said, "It's blocked. You'll have to wait for it to come back."

People were thirsty and wanted water. He couldn't do anything so he left. Some people even died because there was no water. Egypt was a big country and there were over 100 people who died. Then the pharaoh got sick. Everyone was worried. A few days later, the water came back.

Gabriella Swart (9)
The King's House School, Windsor

The Game

One day, there was a man named Bob Billy. Bob had an idea. He wanted to create a thing called a game. He started by carving different pieces of wood. He found that he had one board to play on and a few pieces to move. The game had to have two players. He made loads of games. People wanted to buy them.

Soon, he ran out of games. Then he retired. He didn't have any food. He became very weak so he got up and made more games and soon he became a millionaire and wasn't hungry.

Nathaniel Bramley (9)
The King's House School, Windsor

The Death Of A Hero

Erik, who was the ruler of The Runestones, stared at the endless sea in despair, hoping to see a speck of land. Instead, Erik had situated a long tentacle of a sea creature that grabbed his shipmates into the sea towards land he had never seen before. Immediately, Erik swam like a sailfish to save his friends.

Exploring the unknown, wild island, he spotted tree creatures with huge claws who inhabited the land. Erik fought and fought for his friends, hopeful to save them. Unfortunately, saving his friends led to his death. Darkness consumed him with his arm ripped off.

Muhammed Hassan Saeed (11)
Tudor Primary School, Southall

Liking The Viking

Vikings were people that dressed with horns on their hats. They had some interesting remedies such as onion soup... smelly! When you were twelve, you were an adult. Well, not anymore! They played games like piggy in the middle with bearskin. Well, we have fixed that and have balls. They got ill quickly so changed to fabric, no more skin clothes. They could speak Norse. Impressive! These Vikings were very good fighters so don't fight them. We solved their problems like clothing, games and fighting. You do know they are cleaner than others? Would you like to be one?

Safina Yakub (10)
Tudor Primary School, Southall

Horrid Adventure

In Egypt, the Khufu pyramid was found robbed. Everything was gone! The robber's footprints were in the sand. All I had to do was follow and I'd catch the thief.

After travelling for ages, I found a cabin but the footprints stopped. I had no choice but to go inside the cabin and inside was the thief. I'd found him! The police arrived and used rope to tie him and take him away. I picked up artefacts one by one until they were all back to where they came from. I felt like a hero. I had a party.

Finn Campbell (11)
Walgrave Primary School, Walgrave

World War I

In 1914, a bad war happened. Bombs, tanks and nukes. The war wasn't a good thing. Millions of people died. People with brave and manifesting hearts. People felt trepidation on their back, like electric shivering down their spine. Luckily, Maria was there to help. People thought she was being enthusiastic but she wasn't.
A couple of years went by and she tried to help but she couldn't succeed.

Katy-May Adair (11)
Washingborough Academy, Washingborough

Conquering The Ocean

Standing on the shore, Caligula looked out at the ferocious waves. "I can't conquer Britain," he said. "Men, new orders, now. Britain is only small, we need to conquer something bigger! We will conquer the ocean. Everyone collect as many seashells as you can find!" shouted Caligula. So they started the job and collected as many seashells as they could find while Caligula watched them. They successfully finished and returned back to ancient Rome. "I have conquered the ocean!" Caligula shouted. "I have conquered the ocean!"

Isla Gael Martin (9)
Whitburn Village Primary School, Whitburn

Slave

I was thown into a large boat which carried me across the freezing cold ocean to become a slave. My eyes were wide open but I could just see pitch-black. The horrible smell of dirty rocks and disgusting water floated around, making the place smell terrible. I could hear loud thunder crashing against the ocean. I could feel rock-hard chains around me, tightening my cold thin body. Suddenly, I was hauled into a low stony tomb and locked inside a cramped space. From then on, I was working very hard. My life was terrible for ages...

Izzy Sampson (8)
Wyburns Primary School, Rayleigh

Slaves

One day, I woke up. I had forgotten all about my family. I could see pitch-black. I could hear the pharaohs giving me orders and I heard people crying. I felt scared. "What shall I do?" I tried to run away but they caught me. They dragged me back and I got more orders. What will I do when my boss dies?

I could smell the sandstone under my feet. "Please give me a chance, I'm begging you!" I could feel them dragging me everywhere and pain.

Oh no, what will I do? My boss died. Oh no.

Harry Dodd (8)
Wyburns Primary School, Rayleigh

Slaves

I don't feel too comfortable. I'm lying on the hardest concrete I've ever felt. I cannot see a thing. I feel chains around my arms and legs. I can smell dust and dirty water. I also hear the metal of the chains. I hear other people mumbling, trying to speak. I am keeping quiet. I am stuck in a box on a huge boat. I hear someone shout, "You have no rights!"
There are about twenty of us.
We arrive at a rich-looking pyramid. I miss my family. I am so alone. I need help, please.

Hayden Aylott (9)
Wyburns Primary School, Rayleigh

Help!

I could feel the chains around my arms and legs. I looked at my surroundings. They were herding twenty-five people.
"Ow!" I yelled.
They chucked me into a dirty cage. I could see that the people were really dirty and grimy. I was so sad. I was alone to cry. There were holes in the walls where rats and mice lived. I did the best I could to get a family but I couldn't. It was horrible because I couldn't move or speak. I'm so sad. I only wanted a family. I need help. Please help me.

Isla Brindle (8)
Wyburns Primary School, Rayleigh

Slaves

I was confused when I woke up in an unknown place. I was in a very silent room. I could smell old water from the streams. I could hear bricks being slammed on the floor. I was thrown on a boat with lots of force. To go get some bricks, I was crammed in with 100 other people with no respect. "Help! Help!" I screamed.

I was thrown on the floor to start building. After about an hour, my hands felt like they were gone. I tried to get out but I couldn't. It was as if I wasn't there...

Phoebe Glendinning (8)
Wyburns Primary School, Rayleigh

Slaves

"Ouch!"
I was hurled into a cage. I could hear the rickety sound of chains coming from my ankles. It felt horrible just like being slaves. Oh, wait a second, I am a slave! This is torture. When I'm not working, I'm in a cage. It's so boring. If you were to talk you were killed. Guess what happened to me next... I was hurled into a boat. There was only one boat and 53 slaves. I had no idea all of us were going to sit on the back. My master was killed. I knew my horrible fate.

Hayden R (8)
Wyburns Primary School, Rayleigh

Slaves

I woke up cold. I could smell wet wood. I looked around to see a dirty water bucket. Oh no, what had happened? I stood up and walked around. All I could hear was banging against the wood. It was really cramped. I could barely move. I was thirsty but I didn't want to drink the disgusting, yucky water. I tried so hard not to drink but it was too yucky. I walked around looking for food but nothing. There was no food. No clean water. There was nothing comfy whatsoever. Help! Please help me escape.

Chloe Day (8)
Wyburns Primary School, Rayleigh

Trapped!

As I opened my eyes, I knew I had been captured. I screamed, "Help!" But it was a bad idea because no one could hear me. I tried to get out but the rope was too thick. I could not get out of there. I yelled again, "Help! Help!" I tried again and again. No one could hear me. I was really angry. I heard footsteps up above me. "Help! Help!" I yelled one more time. I tried one more time to break out. I did it. I was so proud of myself. I walked around proud and happy.

Kiki Howell (9)
Wyburns Primary School, Rayleigh

Bang!

I was so cramped. I needed to escape. I could feel the dirty water that was hurting my toes. It was as cold as thin ice. I tried to get the attention of the four people around me but they didn't answer me. We had to be silent. I feel alone. I am so hungry. My tummy is growling. I wish I could hear something.
I could hear an aeroplane. All of a sudden, the boat crashed. "Ouch!" My head hit the floor. I have a headache. I need to get some rest. Help me. Please help!

Tommy Mackenzie (8)
Wyburns Primary School, Rayleigh

The Pharaoh

No! A prisoner has escaped. Catch him! Catch him and get to it! I have to get him back immediately or he will escape from the grounds and release the others to freedom. Get him back right now or else I will get mad. Do you really want to see me mad, do you? Follow my instructions or I will take you to the tomb. Now get on with it and listen to your pharaoh. I am the most special being and you must worship the ground I walk on. Now, where is that servant with my big breakfast?

Ivy Newcombe
Wyburns Primary School, Rayleigh

Slave

There was complete silence everywhere. I slowly opened my eyes. I was in a tiny box. I could hear the waves crashing as we were pulling up on shore.
Walking along the street, people were staring at me. I felt like I was an animal with all cages and chains. When I was in the cage, I felt chains on me. I tried getting out but there was no hope. They were locked with a key. I had to do lots of work. My life was boring. I just wanted to see my mum and dad again.

Sydnee Herrera (9)
Wyburns Primary School, Rayleigh

Slave

I was chucked on a boat to go to my new home. I was scared.

Finally, I was there but before I could do anything I was chucked into a dungeon. When it came to lunch, all I got was gruel.

Yesterday, I had to make a tiny pyramid for a rich family. I got to work. It was hard work. It took an hour to make but I did it. I wish I had rights.

Kamil Quereshi (9)
Wyburns Primary School, Rayleigh

Help!

The gate slammed I felt the ground shaking. Please someone help me. Please don't let me die. There is dirty water. Please help me. I am dying of thirst and I am being treated badly. I don't like this place because if my master dies, I die. It's fair for everyone. My master is mean and cruel. I am scared and frightened.

George (8)
Wyburns Primary School, Rayleigh

YOUNG WRITERS
INFORMATION

We hope you have enjoyed reading this book – and that you will continue to in the coming years.

If you're a young writer who enjoys reading and creative writing, or the parent of an enthusiastic poet or story writer, do visit our website www.youngwriters.co.uk. Here you will find free competitions, workshops and games, as well as recommended reads, a poetry glossary and our blog.

If you would like to order further copies of this book, or any of our other titles give us a call or visit **www.youngwriters.co.uk**.

'HE CAME, HE SAW, HE CONKED US'!

Young Writers
Remus House
Coltsfoot Drive
Peterborough
PE2 9BF

(01733) 890066
info@youngwriters.co.uk

 YoungWritersUK

 @YoungWritersCW